Ask Nothing in Return

by

Jane Drager

Ask Nothing in Return

Cover Art by *Diana Carlile*

The Wild Rose Press, Inc.
PO Box 708
Adams Basin, NY 14410-0708
Visit us at www.thewildrosepress.com

Publishing History
First Crimson Rose Edition, 2014
Print ISBN 978-1-62830-085-7
Digital ISBN 978-1-62830-086-4

Published in the United States of America

With lightning speed, Odessa's arm slipped around Alena's neck, lifting her off the seat and pinning the chair between them. Cold metal pressed against her temple.

Uh-oh.

Two men charged into the room, weapons drawn. One man was Sam, looking angry as hell. "Let her go, Odessa. You're finished!"

"Like hell! You have to let me out of here, or I'll put a bullet through her head!"

Was this how she was destined to die? Survive a stroke but die from a bullet to her brain?

She struggled. Odessa's arm tightened around her throat.

"Stay still, sweetie. You do as you're told, and you'll stay alive. You're my insurance policy."

"Put down the gun. It's over."

Odessa's arm stiffened. Alena sensed the anger in that arm. A man playing an equally cunning game fooled the bitch.

Oh, dear. To hell with the bullet in her brain. Odessa was choking her to death!

Johnny, why did you do this to me? Wasn't my stroke enough?

Alena struggled to draw air into her lungs. She tried to kick her way out of the chair, but Odessa had the strength of a bull elephant. Now what?

"You hurt her, and I will shoot you dead, Odessa."

They were excellent marksmen, right? Professionals go through extensive training. They couldn't possibly miss Odessa and kill her instead.

Odessa's gun hand twitched. The trigger inched back. And then consciousness slipped away.

Also by Jane Drager

SECRETS BY NECESSITY
A Contemporary Romance

Dedication

To my hubby,
who pushed when I wanted to give up.

Chapter One

Sam McCullen stood motionless in a doorway to a semi-lit room. Staff members wearing gray scrubs passed behind him, some pushing gurneys, others wheelchairs with fussy elderly patients trying to get up and walk when they shouldn't. No one stopped to question why he stared enthralled into an x-ray reading room.

A woman doctor was positioned before illuminated panels. She studied a series of x-rays, occasionally lifting a magnifying lens to see more closely. She murmured into a headset microphone, medical jargon that made absolutely no sense. Her voice purred with sensuality, despite being matter-of-fact, the kind of voice that sent shivers of pleasure up a man's spine.

"You're a doctor!" he cried.

It was a stupid thing to say, but he blurted the words before he screwed his brain in tight. Of course, he knew she was a doctor. He knew everything about her—well, almost everything.

The woman turned. Her face reflected neither surprise nor recognition at the behemoth of a man blocking the doorway. "Can I help you?"

"We're neighbors!"

That brought a reaction. Arched eyebrows shot upward.

"We live in the same apartment complex," he

1

explained. "You're from Apartment 115, right? I'm in 418, across the parking lot, second floor. I'm usually on the balcony in the morning with a cup of coffee and newspaper. I watch you leave for work every day." He stepped in and extended his hand. "Sam McCullen."

Uncertainty covered her face. Then, with hesitation, she extended her hand. "Alena Nichols."

Sam had often wondered if the illusion of distance would disappoint if they ever came face-to-face. Surveillance photos never did anyone a bit of justice. They were always snapped from afar without the suspect having a clue. She was a pretty woman without question. Light brown hair, pale brown eyes, fair skin. Now that she stood before him so up close and personal, he felt sucker-punched.

Her voice broke through his thoughts. "Did you have your hand x-rayed?"

He looked at his left hand. "Yeah, it's just a scratch."

"I don't think so, Mr. McCullen. It's turning purple."

He had his suit jacket draped over his left forearm as a nonchalant way of keeping his hand elevated. The damn appendage hurt like hell. He didn't need a medical degree to see the thing was twice its normal size.

"You should have ice on that," she said.

"I'd rather have a cold beer. I can cool it from the inside out."

Sam had done a double-take when he passed. Never in a million years did he expect to meet her this way, but here he was, in need of a hospital and its services. His hand injury proved a lucky break, no pun intended.

She again interrupted his thoughts. "Did you come in through the emergency department?"

"No. A doctor in our office building sent me over. I met him in the elevator."

Alena picked up a phone and punched in numbers. "Michael, a Mr. Sam McCullen had his left hand x-rayed. Will you find the films and bring them to me in the reading room?" She hung up and took his hand. Her touch resembled a caress rather than examination. "How'd you hurt it?"

"Car door."

She grimaced. "Ouch."

"It was my own fault. I was preoccupied." With a woman's ass, unfortunately. He never saw one jiggle so easily.

She released his hand. "How did you recognize me?"

He pointed to the cane on the chair. "There aren't too many attractive women walking around with a cane in their hand. You use it to and from the car, rain or shine."

The comment shot a look of suspicion his way as a young man rushed in carrying a small brown envelope. He gave Sam a quick once-over before turning an adoring gaze on Alena. He handed her the films. "I can wait for them if you'd like," he said with a slight lisp.

His voice pleaded. *Good grief, was he about to drool?*

"Thanks, Michael. No, you don't have to wait."

Michael's face reflected his disappointment. He turned, gave Sam a defiant glare, and left the room.

Alena put Sam's x-rays on the lit panels. She

3

studied them with a deep frown forming on her forehead. "Where were you going after your x-rays, Mr. McCullen?"

"Back to the office."

"Well, you have three breaks: here, here, and here."

She pointed. He acted as if he saw the breaks as clearly as she did. He hadn't a clue really. Bones in black and white. "You'll need a cast. What kind of doctor sent you?"

"Kidneys, I think."

"That was nice of him, but I doubt he has the skill or the supplies to set one. Very likely he would send you back to us."

This was a definite inconvenience. He made a face. "Does it have to be a cast?"

She removed the films from the panel and placed them in the envelope. "I highly recommend it. You should go to our emergency department. Dr. Nan Bauer is on. She's very good with hands." She again got on the phone. "Wendy, are you busy? I want you to take a gentleman to the ED, a Mr. Sam McCullen." She hung up.

Her pale brown eyes swept over him as if assessing his worth. Whether she approved or disapproved, he couldn't tell. In reality, it was plain old curiosity. Sam McCullen had size and strength. He missed the good-looks gene pool in the womb. As a rule, women didn't fall panting at his feet. He puffed his chest out just in case.

"I'll call Dr. Bauer and let her know you're coming," she continued. "Take these x-rays with you." She handed him the brown envelope and ushered him toward the door. "Head down the hall and look for a little redhead. That's Wendy. It was nice to meet you, Mr. McCullen. I'm sorry it had to be under these circumstances."

Sam wasn't sorry at all. He finally met the woman who never noticed him watching from the balcony. Weeks of wonder proved him right after all. She was beautiful. The surveillance photos never showed details, and Alena Nichols had some very nice details.

He stopped to look back at her to see her stop to look back at him. Their eyes met and held. The uncertainty that passed across her face pleased him for some reason. He aroused her interest at least. That helped. He gave her a quick wink before turning to meet up with the little redhead named Wendy.

****

Sam had suffered his share of injuries on his rise to adulthood. He'd seen enough of the inside of an emergency room to know what to expect. He didn't expect the whirlwind of a black woman blowing in without the slightest warning.

She introduced herself as Dr. Nan Bauer with a breath that gushed out to match the wind. While Alena had displayed calm surrounded by her environment of x-rays, Nan Bauer resembled untapped energy. She barked out commands faster than the staff could follow.

Sam soon found himself on a gurney with blue plastic covering his dress trousers. The x-rays went up on lit panels. A computer on wheels was positioned next to his feet. By the time the doctor gathered her supplies and took his hand, she was an ocean of calm.

"Are you a friend of Dr. Nichols?" he asked as she began the process of setting a cast.

"Best friends since med school. We were lucky to get hired by the same hospital." She glanced up. "Why?"

"She's very attractive."

Nan grunted. "A lot of men say that. A lot of good it does, too."

"Why, is she gay?"

"Hardly. Just not interested…yet."

Sam decided not to pursue that particular piece of news for the time being. The last thing he wanted was to have Nan Bauer clam up over some privacy issues. He already knew Alena never had visitors to her apartment, male or female. "You both look too young to be doctors," he said. "Early thirties at a guess."

"Good guess." She eyed him through slits. "Is this your subtle way to find out how old she is?" She stopped with the plaster to glance at his medical chart displayed on the computer screen. "I see from your record that you are thirty-two." She turned back. "Alena's younger than you."

Sam liked Dr. Bauer. She was a direct to-the-point woman. A refreshing trait. Women were so damn pretentious these days. "Dr. Nichols lives in my apartment complex," he explained. "I've seen her lots of times, but we only met today. Is she always so serious?"

"Serious?" Nan stopped to stare into space. "Yes, she is serious. She never used to be."

"Why?"

"You can ask, Mr. McCullen, but I won't answer."

Fair enough. He took a shot and lost. "She probably has a lovely smile."

"It will bowl you over. If you're interested, then

good luck trying. Most men give up."

That surprised him. "Care to elaborate?"

"No. She'll tell you in her own time—provided you stick around long enough. She won't encourage you."

"I have the patience of a saint."

Nan paused to study him. "You thinking of asking her out?"

"It crossed my mind. Is it a good idea?"

"Depends." Nan's dark brown eyes assessed him in one quick sweep. As with Alena, he stuck his chest out for the hell of it. "It might do her good if a man other than a doctor showed some interest," she said. "Do you have any medical training?"

"I can put on a Band-Aid."

She nodded her approval. "You'll do, Mr. McCullen. It won't be easy so give it your best shot. There, finished. How's that feel?"

He held up his hand to inspect her work. "I can't wiggle my fingers."

"That's because wiggling will hurt. You broke two of the bones that control your fingers. Good thing you weren't wearing any rings."

"I haven't worn a ring since—hey, wait a minute! Are you trying to find out if I'm married?"

She grinned. "Your medical record lists divorced so I'm one step ahead of you." She threw off his plastic drape and tossed everything in the trash. She turned to face him, her expression serious. "Do me a favor, Mr. McCullen. If you plan to pursue Alena, please be gentle. She's been hurt enough. As a defense, she's covered her emotions with a protective coating. It's going to take a special man to melt it away."

His brows shot up in surprise. "I'm not a beast,

doc, unless—" He paused. "Does it have anything to do with the cane?"

Nan Bauer's dark eyes flashed. "It has everything to do with that damn cane!" She pushed the computer off to the side. "Sorry. Some things still upset me. Come on. I'll escort you to the exit."

Once back on the street, Sam took out his cell phone. He typed a short message. *Contact made.*

He hit the Send button.

Chapter Two

Alena Nichols thought no more of Sam McCullen until she stepped out the door the following morning. Something drew her gaze across the wide expanse of parking lot to a second floor balcony. There he sat sunning himself with a cup of coffee in his right hand. The left he raised in a wave and motioned to the hot pink cast that immobilized his hand and wrist.

She almost laughed. Hot pink suited him. As proof, he wore an equally bright pink dress shirt. The color emphasized his linebacker build and complemented his cropped blond hair and impressive chest. Without question, the balcony looked way too flimsy to support a man with his weight. She waved back and got in her car.

She ignored the feelings he stirred in her, feelings she hadn't felt in years. All physical and long believed dead. Yesterday, when she had turned to see him standing in the doorway, her insides jolted. He had a presence, something akin to a Goliath towering over his troops. A commanding persona, the type who entered a room and brought all activity to a standstill.

After he left, the feelings he stirred had stayed with her until she buried her mind in work. Seeing him on the balcony rushed those feelings to the forefront again. It was a physical urge, a hormonal surge. Nothing personal. Classic textbook. Female attracted to male for

9

reasons unknown.

Unknown like hell.

Alena arrived at the hospital focused and ready to work.

Or so she thought.

Nan Bauer caught up to her halfway through the parking garage. They entered the elevator together. "Well?" Nan asked. Her brown eyes were wide with anticipation.

Alena looked at her friend, full of energy, full of life. A dynamo in a small package. She pushed the button for the ground floor. "Most people say good morning."

"I want to know what happened."

Alena stared. "With what?"

"The big dude from your apartment complex. You know, the broken hand?"

"Oh, him. Nasty break."

"I'm not talking his injury. Didn't you and Blondie see each other last night?"

"No, of course not."

Nan pouted. "Rats."

They exited the elevator and walked toward the main lobby. "What made you think we'd get together?"

"Hope really. Same apartment complex. Decent looking stud. Nice muscles, too."

Alena stopped in her tracks. "I hope you didn't strip him naked to put on a cast!"

Nan turned with a face full of annoyance. "Give me some credit, Alena." She walked backwards until Alena caught up. "He had nice muscles in his arm. You're the one who should see what the rest looks like."

Alena laughed. "You're incorrigible."

"Well, all he talked about was you."

That surprised her. "Why?"

"Because you're beautiful, dumb-ass. That never changed. You need to start dating again."

"I'm not ready."

Nan grunted. "You won't be ready until you ditch the cane."

"I'm doing fine."

"Yeah, right." She checked her watch. "Gotta run. Let's try to meet for lunch. Baked macaroni is on the menu."

Nan ran off leaving Alena wondering what her friend had up her sleeve this time.

"Dr. Nichols?"

Alena turned to see Joe McMann approach from behind the security counter. Joe was a gangling kind of man, the kind who never quite fit into his uniform. No matter what he wore, he never looked good in it.

"Hi, Joe. What's new?"

He walked alongside. "Extra security cameras were installed in your department last night. State of the art stuff."

"Why? It's only x-ray."

"Orders from above. Never know these days."

True, but she could think of better areas for new cameras besides a boring x-ray department.

"If you ever have any trouble, you make sure you call me right away," he said. "I've got a bird's eye view of your department now."

"Okay, Joe, thanks."

Call the beanpole? The man who looked all skin and bones? She wasn't sure Joe had the strength to fight his way out of a paper bag. Unlike Sam McCullen. Now, that man looked capable of crushing another man with one pinkie.

A nice thought.

She stepped into the elevator. The mail clerk pushing his mail cart joined her.

"I saw Joe talking to you," he said when the doors closed. "Hate to break it to you, doc, but the guy has the hots for you."

Great. Another wonderful piece of news. "I hope he didn't tell you that."

"Not in so many words, but a man knows these things. He wanted to deliver your mail personally. That's so he could see your pretty face. I told him it was against the rules."

"Thank you." Like she wanted the beanpole panting at her heels. Hell, he was practically a baby.

She stepped off the elevator at her floor.

So much for focus.

Remembering Joe's news, she glanced at the overhead camera. Nothing new about that one. Cobwebs covered the lens since housekeeping never bothered to use the dust wand up there. The one down the end of the hall wasn't new either.

He said extra cameras, not new ones.

Extra where?

She did a double-take when she entered her office. They'd installed a camera in the corner ceiling!

She hurried to the reading room and saw one positioned in the far corner. On a whim, she inspected her boss' office. Then another radiologist office. Neither had a camera. For the hell of it, she checked the bathroom. Nothing. Why the reading room? Why her office?

She called Joe. He ran in half breathless.

She pointed to the camera staring at her desk. "Get it out."

"I can't do that, ma'am. Orders from above."

"There's a patient confidentiality issue at stake, Joe. I can't have a camera in here. Remove it or get administration to explain why they want it."

She recognized a shit-ass order when she heard it. No one in their right mind would breach the patient confidentiality ruling.

Joe bit his lip, his face a mask of indecision. He got his orders from someone, and it wasn't from above. Even her boss wouldn't be dumb enough to put in such an order.

"Why my office, Joe, and none of the other doctors?"

"I do what I'm told, ma'am."

A stock answer. She suppressed a growing irritation. "I'll accept the camera in the reading room, stupid as it is, but not here. And there better not be any placed in the patient areas."

"No, ma'am. We installed the two last night. I'll disconnect this one."

"No, you will remove it. I can't have patients see a camera in my office. I want it out within the hour. Do I make myself clear?"

She never pushed her weight around. As a rule, she was docile and compliant, never an argument out of her mouth, always striving to stay calm in a world of chaos. In fact, the last time she put her foot down was with her mother, and that was a very long time ago.

After Joe removed the camera, Carol, the

department receptionist, popped her head in. She glanced up at the mess Joe made of the ceiling. "There was no work order for this, Dr. Nichols. Shall I inform Dr. Hoffman when he arrives?"

"Yes, tell him I'm not pleased." She'd talk to him personally if and whenever he dragged his butt to work. Half the time, she missed him because he ran off to a meeting.

"By the way, there's a gentleman out here who says he's your fiancé's father. Shall I send him back?"

Alena started. "Johnny's father?" What could he want after all these years? They had never met while Johnny was around, so this visit raised her curiosity up a notch. "Send him in, Carol."

Johnny was a part of her life that she wanted to erase from memory. But really now, how could she when the incident was so ingrained into her current lifestyle?

An elderly man walked in. Nondescript. Not good-looking but not bad-looking either. He dressed like he had money, which he did. His son had never seen any of it.

She spoke first. "What can I do for you?"

"I understand you were engaged to my son."

"That's right with the emphasis on the past tense."

"I want to know where he is."

Yeah, wouldn't we all.

"I can't help you, Mr. Goodhart. Johnny left a long time ago." The pain came out with the words. She cleared her throat. "I take it you're here in Philadelphia on business."

He ignored the statement. "You must have an idea where he is."

"Living and breathing somewhere on the planet, I suppose." The words sounded callous, but hey, she was human. "Why the interest all of a sudden? He told me you disowned him."

"I don't like people probing into my affairs because of some asinine stunt he pulled."

A curious statement. She cocked her head. "Care to elaborate?"

"I can't elaborate on something I don't understand. I've got people right and left asking questions about him, probing into my finances and my personal life. I don't like it."

No, he wouldn't like it. He was a successful businessman slash politician. From what little she knew about him, his political connections were questionable.

"I can't help you, Mr. Goodhart. Johnny left me over two years ago. I haven't heard from him since. If someone is looking for him, there must be a reason why."

"If I had the answer to that, I wouldn't be here."

"All right then, *who's* asking about Johnny?"

The fire alarm blared. "Condition Red. Third floor."

The elderly man covered his ears. "Christ, that's loud!"

"Yes," she shouted. "Stay here. I have protocol to follow." And protocol was to close every door along the hall. She met up with Carol who came down the other end closing doors along the way. They met in the middle holding their ears.

Finally, the alarm stopped.

"Condition Green," came over the loud speaker.

"Thank God for small favors," Carol declared.

"I'm deaf."

They retraced their steps, opening doors as they passed.

Alena opened the door to her office. The room was empty. She searched the hall. He had to pass her if he left by the stairwell. Where did he go? And who was asking about a man she wanted to forget?

Chapter Three

A gorgeous Saturday afternoon pulled Alena out of her apartment like a magnet attracting its mate. She couldn't resist. Spring was in the air. Flowers had popped through the soil. Tree buds had burst into colorful little blossoms. The air fresh, crisp, and full of pollen. The latter meant allergy season and an abundance of sinus x-rays from here on through summer. Job security for sure. She strolled to the park adjacent to the apartment complex.

People crowded the wide asphalt path that circumvented a small lake. Some walked briskly with weights in their hands. Others jogged. Kites flew overhead. A father and son tossed a baseball back and forth. Springtime activities that were always a joy to see.

Two girls zipped by on roller-blades. Alena made a quick sidestep to avoid them. The maneuver put her in full view of the curve in the path. She spotted Sam McCullen coming around the bend.

She couldn't miss him. His hot pink cast caught her eye, as did his bright yellow shirt reflecting equally bright sunshine. He looked like a walking flowerbed. Instincts told her to bolt and run. Instincts and bad memories. She didn't want another encounter with a man she couldn't dismiss. Common sense convinced her to stay put. Most men wouldn't bother with a woman using a cane. They preferred the spontaneous jump-in-the-sack kind of woman, one without the hang-ups that curtailed her life. She sat on a bench away from the path to wait for him to pass.

Women provided a constant distraction as he walked. They ogled the well-defined muscles on his chest and arms. They ogled his ass. He ambled on powerful legs, allowing time for every female to turn and admire.

Though not particularly handsome, he was attractive in his own way with blond hair the color of pale daisies and hazel eyes that sparkled brighter than polished gems. Since everyone in the park—herself included—emerged from the winter doldrums with washed-out complexions, Sam looked like a poster boy for good health with his tanned skin and fat-free body.

The bench rattled. A man flopped next to her. A little too close for her comfort. She shifted over.

"Don't go far, doctor. I don't want to talk loud."

She stared at the small, weaselly man with a face covered with overlapping wrinkles. His breath smelled like cheap cigarettes, and his skin had the ashen color of a man not long for the world. Yet, he wasn't old. Forty at a guess.

"Give us what we want, doctor. It's in your best interest."

Her mouth fell open. "I beg your pardon?"

A pair of furtive eyes shifted in every direction. "It won't do you any good to hang onto it. Give it to me now, and I'll leave."

"You must have me mistaken for someone else."

"No mistake. You've got it, and we want it." He coughed, a loose bronchitic hack that precipitated into an uncontrollable fit.

"You're smoking too much," she said. Either that or he had TB.

"You're playing a dangerous game," he said. "A pretty doctor like you could get hurt." He jumped to his feet and ran off.

Alena stared after him.

"Was he bothering you?" a man asked.

Sam McCullen stood alongside the bench like a bull ready to charge.

"I think you scared him," she said, puzzled. "He wanted me to give him something."

"What?"

She scratched her head. "He never said, but thanks for interrupting. He gave me the creeps."

What the hell was happening to her? First, an unauthorized camera in her office. Then, Johnny's father who showed up out of the blue. Now, a stranger demanding…what?

"It's good I was walking by," Sam said. "I like coming to a woman's rescue. Enjoying the sun?"

"I'm getting my weekly dose of Vitamin D." No exaggeration. She spent ten hours a day inside a dark room, sunup to sundown. Small wonder her bones didn't crumble. "You can come to my rescue anytime, Mr. McCullen." Shit. Did she really say that?

"You were going to let me pass without saying hello," he said with a slight pout. "That wasn't nice."

The man spoke with a gravelly voice as if pebbles bounced around on his vocal cords. Like his linebacker build, the sound fit.

"How's the hand?" she responded.

He moved the tips of his fingers to show he could.

"Hurts." He sat on the bench. The movement knocked her cane to the ground. He picked it up and shook it a few times as if assessing its weight. "Nice cane. Solid walnut. A good weapon." He rested it against the bench.

"My grandfather made this cane," she said while touching it. "He hand-carved the handle while listening to baseball games." She never contemplated using it so early in life either. "Where are you from, Sam?"

He groaned and dropped his chin onto his chest. "I knew it. It's obvious."

"Let's say the rest of us are still a little pale. Come on. Fess up."

"I'm from California. LA to be exact. I transferred out here six weeks ago."

"Then Philadelphia is quite a change for you. What made you decide here?"

He shrugged. "It happened."

All right. Not the best conversation continuum. She stared at the lake.

"Sorry, doc. I finally have a chance to talk to you, and I clam you up with something stupid."

"It happens." She threw the words right back at him.

How long had he watched her from the balcony? If he wore hot pink and bright yellow shirts, she had to be blind not to see him. Preoccupation no doubt. A desire to blend in unnoticed. Also a desire to remain uninvolved. Yet, she knew she couldn't live the rest of her life as a hermit. It wouldn't be healthy.

She looked at him and found him looking at her. There was something very comfortable about the man. His eyes had warmth. They had interest. And something else. Curiosity maybe. She felt curiosity, too. She cleared her throat and looked back at the lake. "You can call me Alena."

"Good because I fully intend to. I'm glad you remembered my name."

She looked at him again and watched his lips curl into a smile. A nice smile, the kind that threw a woman off guard. Sexy. Warm. Enticing. He was doing a damn good job throwing her for a loop. *Hmmm. Keep it casual; keep it light. Don't let him get too close.* Warnings she repeated in her head like a needle stuck in a record groove. "Do you like your apartment?" A safe subject. That and water pipes.

"I'd rather have a house. I feel too big for an apartment." He sat back and stretched his arm across the backrest. His hand reached to her shoulders, infringing into her space. She fought the urge to sit forward.

"I have to give my new job a chance before I decide if I like it enough to stay," he continued. "Then I'll think about a house. Maybe a condo. Something bigger than what I have anyway. How long have you lived here?"

"Oh, coming up on seven months. It suits my needs perfectly." Small, easy to maintain…no steps. "I'm hardly home long enough to feel the need for something better."

A soccer ball rolled his way. With a simple lift of his leg, he kicked the ball back to a little boy.

"My bank is three blocks from your hospital," he stated.

She shifted on the bench to face him. "You work in a bank?"

The words were more an incredulous statement than a question. He grinned in response. "Yes, I know. I don't look the type. And no, I am not security. I have an MBA in finance. Got that on a football scholarship."

His linebacker build confirmed the football career. Every big man she knew had played football. But a banker? He looked more like a bouncer. "Were you aiming for a pro career?"

"Nay. I wasn't interested. I wanted to make money without destroying every joint in my body. I made a ton of money as a stockbroker, but it ultimately ruined my marriage."

"Too bad."

He crossed his legs. "My own fault really. I was never home. My wife got into loose sex and drugs out of sheer boredom. She hated me for what she became and made my life miserable. We divorced six months ago. No kids." He brushed pieces of grass off the bottom of his pant leg. "My ex hounded me after our divorce. She got so bad, I decided to leave LA and start a new life. I never expected to move to the east coast, but I got an offer that sounded perfect. So, I moved out here and took a position as president of the corporate department at Mutual Bancorp. A nine-to-five job. Straight salary. No bonuses. No commissions—"

"No excitement."

He smirked. "Right. A duller than dirt job."

"I guess you won't stay long then."

"Actually, I told myself I needed to give the job a good try. It's a prestigious position, I'll admit. The money's good—hours are great, and I get comp time. It gives me room to breathe. That's important." He leaned forward and put his elbows on his knees. His gaze followed two joggers on the path. "I realize being alone doesn't help how I feel at times. My family and friends are back on the west coast, but I'm slowly making new friends. Like you, Alena." He looked at her. "I'd like to call you a friend. I could use some help with things."

She peered at him. "What kind of things?"

"You know, where to shop, a good mechanic, maybe a great place to take a date, all that. You've got to know your way around better than I do." He sat back.

The man wanted a platonic relationship. A first. Most men tried to get her in bed without any semblance of a date—well, before the cane anyway. She obviously misread the expression of interest on his face. *Slipping, girl, slipping.* Or she was so friggin' out of practice, she forgot what interest looked like. Still, his suggestion was worth considering. This relaxed her to no end, and she smiled.

"I can be your friend provided you ask no more than that," she said.

"Trust me, doc. After a nasty divorce, the last thing I want is to get involved with another woman. I'd rather keep everything free and easy and ask nothing in return if that's okay with you."

"Free and easy sounds good. You can call me a friend."

"Great." He slapped his knee for emphasis. "With that said, how about having an early dinner with me? There's a restaurant a few blocks from here called Luigi's. Ever been there?"

"No. I think it only opened a few months ago."

"Then we'll try it together. Dutch treat."

"I don't have my wallet."

"In that case, you'll owe me. Are you willing?"

Alena hesitated. The extent of her male companionship involved a quick lunch with a male colleague to discuss a case. Strictly business and usually in the hospital cafeteria. Sam wasn't a doctor. He was a man who stirred up her dormant hormones with one sweep of his gaze, a gaze that was expressive and warm. Was it possible to have a platonic relationship with a man who already aroused her interest?

She hesitated too long.

"I'm sorry, Alena. I wasn't thinking. Maybe it's too far to walk."

She looked down at her cane, her constant companion for two years now. "No, it's not far." All right, so she committed herself. She grabbed her cane and stood to her feet. "I'll pay you when we get back."

"Great!" He shot to his feet. "Maybe over dinner, you can give me the name of a good family doctor. I need to change the one on my insurance plan. The people at work tell me he's a real quack."

The man wanted a platonic relationship. *She* wanted a platonic relationship. They carried scars from prior relationships, and the safest course was a light and casual friendship. So why did she feel so irritable about it?

She needed to have her head examined.

Chapter Four

Alena and Sam walked the quiet streets toward the restaurant, chatting as they went. He kept pace with her more than she with him since his stride exceeded anything she could imitate. They discussed the differences between the east and west coasts, the fashions and climate. Small talk really. Nothing personal or probing. The way she liked it.

Alena whirled. The weasel put her on edge, dammit.

"What's the matter?" Sam asked.

"I'm constantly feeling like someone is following me."

Sam searched up and down the street. "I don't see anyone."

"I never see anyone either, but this feeling has been with me for weeks. I can't shake it." Maybe she was losing her mind. She hadn't one scrap of evidence for who or why someone would follow her.

Aside from the weasel man anyway.

The neighborhood surrounding the apartment complex was one of single-family homes of various shapes and sizes. Old oak trees shaded the sidewalks, their roots lifting the walkway to create crooked skateboard ramps. Some houses had well-kept lawns, some had flower gardens, still others with nothing but asphalt and stones. A lovely place to take a stroll with a man who was easy to talk to.

"If you don't mind my asking," he said, "why the cane? It's not like you limp when you walk."

He finally asked. Most men wanted to know sooner rather than later what they were up against. That way, they could decide if the woman was worth the time. "It's to beat big guys like you senseless."

"Oh, I get it. It's so you can have your way with me." His smile broadened. "I'm game."

Her eyes turned into slits. "I doubt any woman can force herself on a man your size."

"Strip yourself naked, and you'll see how much resistance I've got."

That did it. She burst out laughing.

"That brought a smile to your face," he said with a big grin. "You have a beautiful smile, Alena. I say that because you are way too serious. I suspect it has something to do with the cane."

The smile disappeared, and she nodded. "The cane is for balance. Sometimes when I get overly tired, my left leg collapses."

"Car accident?"

"No." She hoped her tone finalized the conversation. She really didn't want to tell him yet.

"Your turn to fess up, Alena. I'm forcing you to talk."

"Why?"

"Because I see sadness on your face. I want to make it disappear."

Why should he care? More important, why should she tell him? Her sadness cut deep into her soul and was too personal to tell a complete stranger. They just met, dammit!

She peeked up to find his hazel gaze full of warmth. And something else. Softness. The man was a gentle Goliath.

"Stroke," she muttered.

Damaged goods. The words had flashed onto the face of every man she told. She refused to look up and see it on Sam's face as well. When he said nothing, she elaborated. "It was actually a blown aneurysm. The aftereffects are the same as a stroke."

"You're a little young for that, aren't you?"

"Strokes and aneurysms can occur at any age, Sam. I'm lucky to be alive."

He grunted. "You should say that last statement with a little more conviction. You don't feel lucky at all, do you?"

"Very perceptive of you. No, I don't feel lucky. I woke up to a living hell."

They walked around two little boys tunneling into the cracks on the sidewalk. They found that task more fascinating than the toy trucks by their knees.

She glanced over her shoulder since the feeling of being followed remained.

"I think you're safe with me," he said.

She *did* feel safe, from the moment he showed up at the bench.

"How long ago did this stroke happen?" Sam asked.

"Two years. It took me a while to get back to work. My left leg remains weak to this day. Nan—that's Dr. Bauer—has been pushing me to enter this intensive rehab program."

"And?"

She kicked a stone. "I've been putting it off."

"Because you have no reason to ditch the cane."

Alena bristled. The comment cut deep, and resentment surfaced. *How dare he*! He knew nothing about her, her struggles, her tears. Like so many men before him, he passed judgment without facts, and it wasn't right. When her head snapped toward him, only a face full of kindness looked back. Her reaction was a defensive one, a practiced art these days. Still…

"You almost got my cane up your ass," she said. She'd spent the last two years maintaining a forced calm. Yet, the other day, she had blown up at Joe. Now, this. Why all of a sudden? Nothing was different in her life.

Except Sam.

A ridiculous notion. She looked away. "I'll ditch the cane when I'm ready." She said the words with finality.

"Once you strengthen the leg you mean."

"Yes." She spoke so softly, she hardly heard herself.

"Then after you recovered, you moved into our apartment complex."

"Right. I needed a ground floor apartment. I don't handle steps well."

"But once you strengthen your leg, that inability should disappear as well."

Damn him. Whatever happened to subtlety? She should tell him to take his friendship and shove it. She didn't need him, and she didn't need another friend. *Men and their friggin' bluntness.* He saw through her, and it grated her nerves raw. *Oh, calm down. Nothing will come of this.* "I'm not ready, Sam."

"No one's rushing you. I'm certainly not, but I

guess I can't invite you up to my place for dinner. I make a mean taco."

A half-grin twisted her lips. "I wouldn't accept anyway."

Who needed whom for a friend here? She told Sam McCullen more about herself in thirty minutes than the sum of two years to any man. She must remind herself to keep her mouth shut.

"Why don't you have a man in your life, Alena?"

So much for keeping her mouth shut. He wanted to push buttons until she exploded. "Too personal, Sam."

"I can't believe you would forego a personal life to dedicate a career in medicine."

She stared. "Where did you get that idea?"

"You can't tell me the cane scares men away. You're too beautiful for such a lame excuse."

"It's not an excuse. It's a fact."

"You're beautiful and available. What more could a guy ask for? Big deal, you have a cane. You must be keeping them away for a reason."

Like talking to a brick wall, and the brick wall was too easy to talk to. Why did she drop her shield when she practiced such reserve for so long? He was no different from other men. "There's no man in my life for the same reason there is no woman in yours."

"Yeah, but I went through a nasty divorce. I still have a bitter taste in my mouth about it. What's your excuse?"

She glared up at him. "Are you always this blunt?"

"I hate beating around the bush. It wastes time and effort."

Alena stopped. She waited for Sam to turn and look back before she spoke. "Do you see this house?"

She pointed.

They stood on the sidewalk before a large Victorian house of blue and gold. A young child rocked in an oversized rocker on the front porch while a dog dug up a freshly planted flowerbed on the front lawn. Sam gave her a quizzical look.

"I had a second story apartment not too far from here before my stroke. Everyday on my way to work, I passed this house. I loved it. When it finally went up for sale, my fiancé and I put in a bid along with a half dozen other people. You should see the inside, Sam. The rooms are hardwood floors, carved wallboards, a perfect size in every way. In the dining room is a fireplace with a built-in mirror surrounded by an awesome ornate wood frame. The man who built the house was a skilled carpenter. You see his work everywhere including the gingerbread on the perimeter of the roof. The owners accepted our bid. I think I floated for a week after that."

Alena continued up the street. Sam stared at the house until he realized she was almost to the corner. He hurried alongside.

"Go on," he insisted.

They walked another half block before she spoke. "My aneurysm blew. When I regained consciousness, he was gone."

Sam stopped walking and stared. "Your fiancé left you?"

She turned to face him, eyes dry, head high. "Now you understand why I don't have a man in my life. His abandonment at such a critical time scarred me deeper than my stroke. Nan broke the news to me. I wanted to curl up and die right then and there because it hurt so bad."

"The guy was a ass, Alena. He obviously didn't love you enough to stick around."

"Obviously." She started walking.

He caught up. "Did he give you an explanation?"

"I never saw him again. He cleaned out his apartment and left, no forwarding address, nothing. He could be in Tibet for all I know." She walked around a tricycle. "You did the same to your wife, Sam. You abandoned her by making your job more important."

"It's not the same thing."

"Isn't it?" She faced him. "You told me you were never home. What would you call it?"

"Working. There's a big difference between working and walking out on someone lying in a hospital bed. Didn't he even leave a note?"

She shook her head. "It's a hard pill to swallow when you believe someone loves you only to find out otherwise. I guess his guilt was more powerful than his love."

Sam started. "Guilt? Is there something you're not telling me?" He caught her arm. "What else happened, Alena?"

She already told him too much. She couldn't possibly tell him the rest without the heart-wrenching pain returning. "Let's say that it will be a while before I give my heart to another man."

His face showed the acceptance of her statement. He caressed her arm before dropping his hand to his side. They continued up the street in silence.

He didn't push. For that, she was thankful. Her trust in men had hit a new low because of her fiancé, and she wasn't sure if she could trust one again. Only time would give her an answer.

"My fiancé's father came to see me the other day," she continued. "I'd never met the man while we were engaged, so his visit was a surprise. He said people were looking for his son."

"What'd you tell him?"

"I couldn't help him. He disappeared before I found out who."

"What do you mean disappeared?"

She explained. "Maybe he realized he was wasting his time."

The whole incident baffled her. She wanted to know who was looking for Johnny and why. Not like she gave a damn anymore. Johnny was gone, and she had put her life back together without him.

After another block, Sam spoke. "It's good we agreed to be friends. We'll follow the handbook on friendship and keep each other company."

She looked at him, puzzled. "What handbook?"

"You know, the one we receive as kids."

She chuckled and looked away. "What a bull-shitter you are."

They stood before the entrance to Luigi's Restaurant, a mom and pop establishment complete with red and white checkered tablecloths. The scent of rich tomato sauce filled the air along with garlic and just a hint of sausage. All from an exhaust fan on the side of the building.

Sam stopped her from entering by taking hold of her shoulders and turning her toward him. He took her chin in his hand and lifted. His finger brushed along her jaw line creating a flood of goose bumps. Something stirred deep within her chest, a familiar but unwanted feeling. She fought like mad to push the emotion away. An impossible feat. A vulnerable moment, she thought with irritation. Nothing more than that.

"You shared some bitter memories with me, Alena. That is the start of a very nice friendship."

"Is that in the handbook, too?"

"I won't let you enter the restaurant with a serious face. You and I both went through some unhappy times, and we need to move on. I'm saying this for my benefit as well as yours. So, as your newfound friend, I shall make it my mission to see you smile. I expect you to do the same for me. Agreed?"

Well, this was different. She never had a platonic relationship with a man, but Sam McCullen made her reconsider the possibilities. He offered strength and support, something she lacked. She met his gaze. "Agreed."

"Good. We'll start with food. Do you like mushrooms on pizza?"

"I *love* mushrooms on pizza!"

With a bow, Sam opened the restaurant door and waved her in.

Chapter Five

Alena ignored Sam for two weeks. At least that was his interpretation. She left for work before sunrise every morning well before he put himself on the balcony, and she came home after dark every night. He resisted the urge to sit out and wait for her. That would be too obvious even by his standards. She had revealed far more than she wanted, a certainty he couldn't dismiss. Yet, she held back, another certainty. He saw it in her face. To get her talking again could prove downright impossible.

Sam kept his appointment with Dr. Nan Bauer despite her suggestion that he seek the skills of a hand specialist. Awkward as it was to wait in a crowded emergency room, wild horses couldn't change his mind. Nan Bauer knew Alena Nichols. Sam wanted to hear every detail about the forlorn radiologist who constantly drifted into his dreams.

"Your swelling is down substantially," Nan said while studying his x-rays, "and your bones are fusing nicely."

She had removed his cast to examine the underlying tissue. A technician took a new set of x-rays, which Nan hung alongside his old set. Satisfied, she opened a drawer and turned toward him, her hands full of colored rolls of plaster cast for his selection. "Do you want another hot pink cast? Or how about lime green?"

He studied her selection with a disheartened knot swelling inside his gut. "Do I still need a cast?"

"I highly recommend it. I said the bones were fusing nicely. That doesn't mean they're healed."

Great. Just what he needed. More inconvenience. His boss had contemplated replacing him because of the injury, but Sam had presented a convincing argument. In truth, it was the best thing that had happened.

He scrunched his face while considering the colors. "Maybe I should pick a more subdued color. I have a formal affair to attend this weekend."

"Then how about black?"

Perfect. It matched his mood.

While she wrapped his hand, he wondered how to broach the subject of Alena without activating Nan's defenses. Best friends took care of each other. Best friends also told each other secrets. Nan knew Alena's secrets. Sam wanted to know them as well. If Alena wouldn't tell him, maybe Nan could.

"Taking a date, Mr. McCullen?"

"No date. My boss is forcing me into this." Like he had all the time in the world to socialize with a bunch of bankers. "As soon as I can, I'll cut out. I don't want to short-change a date."

"A wise decision. No woman wants to buy an expensive gown just to say hello and goodbye."

Sam watched her wrap the plaster. Then, what the hell. "Alena's working too much."

"I've noticed."

"Do you have any idea why?"

"She tells me she's behind in her work. I don't believe that for a second." She stole a glance at him. "I suspect she's avoiding someone."

He frowned. "Namely me."

"Well, I can't say that for sure, but she told me how the two of you fought over the mushrooms on the pizza."

His face brightened. "I let her win."

"You got her out, Sam. That by itself was a big step. She had a good time and won't admit it."

"Too good, I guess. Now, she's avoiding me. What is she afraid of?"

Nan took her time answering. She rearranged some of the plaster wrap as if she were sculpting a statue. "You," she said finally. "Specifically, your gender. Involvement." A long pause. "Closeness."

His frown returned. "All this is because of her fiancé, isn't it?"

Nan grunted. "My oath of 'Do No Harm' will fly right out the window if I ever get my hands on the man. The bastard was packed and out of the state before she opened her eyes. *I* had to tell her, Sam. Those were the hardest words from my mouth. It was awful."

"Did he really move out of state?"

She shrugged while tugging on the plaster wrap. Her irritation transferred to his hand. He winced.

"I don't know where he went," she said through tight teeth. "All I know is he isn't practicing medicine in this state. He hasn't renewed his license." She stopped with the plaster to look at him. Her eyes flashed with anger. "I went to his apartment after four nights of no-show. The damn place was cleaned out. He left without a word, without a note. Nothing. I can't believe he did that to her."

"The guy was a jerk."

"Hmmpf. I have a harsher opinion of the man."

A nurse entered with an armload of supplies. She and Nan chatted while the supplies went into their respective cabinets. Sam hardly listened. As usual, his mind drifted to the doctor in radiology.

"How much did Alena tell you?" Nan asked when the nurse left.

"She showed me the house, how they lost it because of her stroke, and how he disappeared before she woke up. Nothing more than that."

"Consider yourself lucky. That's a lot coming out of her mouth. She hardly says two words about it." Nan stood back to admire her work. "All done. How's it feel? I let your fingers stick out a little more."

He wiggled the tips. "Not enough, doc. I still can't put on a tie."

"Then your casual days have been extended thanks to me. If you need one for your tux, you might consider a clip-on bowtie."

Sam grimaced. "Men do not wear clip-on bowties." He had no idea what to do about his tie. Maybe go without. He had a damn good excuse. "I got the distinct impression that there was more to Alena's fiancé story."

"You have no idea."

"You know, don't you?"

"We're best friends. Of course, I know. She'll tell you the rest when she's ready." She paused, her face thoughtful while staring at his cast. "Lime green would have set your tux off beautifully, Sam." She gathered the trash and dumped it. When she turned back, her eyes grew guarded. "I tend to be protective of Alena. We've been friends for a long time, and I've seen her go to hell and back. I want her to be happy again."

"I can use some suggestions."

Nan studied him. As on the first day they met, her eyes assessed him in one quick sweep. "She'll be a challenge."

"I'm always up to a challenge."

"Most men wouldn't bother."

"I think she's worth the effort."

That satisfied her. She nodded. "I would infiltrate her life. Do it slow and natural. Be her friend but don't push. If you ask her out, she'll say no. So try to do things that she won't label a date." She turned toward the computer. "In other words, let her get used to you being there and doing different things together. Your Dutch treat for pizza was a great way to start."

She typed a few notes on his medical chart. Finished, she turned to him with a serious face. "Under no circumstances should you get me involved. She'll think I'm conniving again, which I am. I want her to enjoy life the way she used to. I've a strange feeling you're the man to help her."

"I'll do my best."

He had seen the sadness in Alena's eyes the second they met in the dark x-ray room. The sadness hovered even while they laughed over the mushrooms. Her problems with her fiancé cut deep into her core and destroyed the spirit of a vibrant woman. Maybe time could revive it, but time was something he did not have.

Sam slipped off the gurney as his cell phone chirped to indicate a text message. He read. *Pkg found SB ACX. Call for details.*

He frowned.

"Bad news?" Nan asked.

"I wish people would realize that I'm new to the east coast. I have no idea where ACX is."

Nan laughed. "Atlantic City Expressway more likely. It's in New Jersey. Fast route to the shore. I haven't driven it in years because I haven't been to a beach in years." She gave him a sheepish look. "It's an isolated road. I avoid it."

An isolated road was an excellent place to lose a package. He had a pretty good guess what that package was.

He followed Nan out of the room.

****

Alena had made a habit of pampering herself every Saturday night. First, a long, soaking bath loaded with bubbles. Sometimes a pedicure, often a manicure. Then curling up on the sofa in pajamas with a good book or movie. This simple ritual had become a necessity after her stroke. It helped ease the pang of loneliness for a fiancé who left without a word. *Damn you, Johnny.* She would never forgive him no matter how much time passed.

Alena stood in the kitchen debating whether to open a bottle of wine or microwave a big bowl of popcorn. She deserved both. She reached for the wine bottle when the doorbell rang. A quick glance at the wall clock showed seven thirty. She rarely had visitors these days. Her own choice. She preferred the quiet life, a life without excitement and hassles. A post-stroke requirement, half-afraid another would strike and kill her. Ridiculous, of course.

She took a quick peek through the door's peephole. Her brows shot up when she saw who waited on the other side. She opened the door.

Sam fidgeted on the step semi-dressed in a black tuxedo. His face showed a combination of irritation and annoyance. To her, he looked drop-dead gorgeous. He held the jacket, cummerbund, and black tie out to her. "I need help!"

"What's the matter?" She ushered him in.

"I need another hand!" He forced her to take the three items from his hand then reached into his trouser pocket. He pulled out a cufflink and handed it to her. He waved his dangling right sleeve. "I can't get myself dressed!"

"Poor baby." She said it with a laugh, took the cufflink, and fastened the sleeve. "There's no way you'll get a cufflink on your left sleeve, Sam."

"No, I'll leave it." He grabbed the bowtie from her and dangled it.

She stared. "I don't know how to do a bowtie."

"I'll show you if you give me a chair and a mirror."

Alena put his jacket and cummerbund on the sofa and placed him in a kitchen chair. She hurried to the bedroom for her hand mirror then shoved it in his hand. Working from behind, she followed his careful instructions—four times—until a decent bowtie emerged.

A mass of confusion surfaced while she worked. She blamed his intoxicating aftershave, which stimulated visions of a romp in bed. She also blamed their up-close-and-personal proximity, a rarity these days where men were concerned. To make matters worse, the gentle brush of her breast against the back of his head triggered a dormant libido that nearly did her in. The stimulus he caused was like throwing a switch. One look, boom, panting. When she finished, she backed away.

"You got it that time, Alena." He inspected it. "Yes, very nice. By the way, I like your pajamas." He sat looking at her in the mirror.

Her pajamas were silk, another part of her Saturday night ritual. She wore no robe. It never entered her mind to throw one on.

Sam stood to his feet, grabbed the cummerbund, and tossed it to her. He sucked in his gut with an exaggerated gasp, but the cummerbund fit perfectly. She helped him on with his jacket.

"You look very handsome, Sam." She brushed lint that wasn't there and straightened his bowtie. That breathless feeling returned. She wasn't sure what rolled around in her chest, but it felt damn good. "What's the occasion?"

"The bank CEO is throwing this fancy anniversary party for his wife," he said with disgust. "It was 'requested' that I attend. I'm already late."

"You better go then. Your date will be furious."

"No date. I'm going stag. If they don't like it, that's too bad. I can always say I got lost." He headed for the door. He stopped and turned. "Alena—"

She looked up, puzzled by the hesitant tone in his voice. Then she cocked her head. "You need help getting undressed?"

His eyes turned into slits. "Coming from you, that sounds downright provocative. Yes, I need help getting undressed, and it took my unfortunate dilemma to finally bring a sparkle to your eyes. Do you realize your iris is the color of desert sand?"

She laughed. "Leave it to a guy from California to tell me that odd piece of news. Maybe you won't need my help. You might get lucky at the party."

"Maybe. I'm not counting on it." He opened the door. "What time do you go to bed?"

"If you need help, Sam, I'll wait up. If you get lucky, call me." She gave him her cell number, which he punched into his phone. He returned the gesture by giving her his cell number.

"All right," she said, with authority, "you're late. Get going." She shooed him out the door.

His aftershave lingered. She closed her eyes and sucked it in, feeling that dormant libido flare up again. The man created too much stimulus. She must remind herself that they had agreed to be friends. Nothing more.

Chapter Six

Sam stood by the curb staring at the subtle lights seeping through the draperies in Alena's apartment. Should he bother her? It had passed the point of midnight an hour ago. He'd stayed at the party a lot later than he wanted, but he couldn't gracefully leave without insulting the boss' daughter. The woman had hung on him like a hanger. He played the coat rack on other jobs, but this one was harder for some reason. Maybe he was getting tired of it.

A strange statement. No, he wasn't tired of his job. It offered excitement, travel, and above all, money. How could he tire of that?

His ex-wife had enjoyed the money. She depleted his bank account after every job. He enjoyed the danger, too. Just like his father. His old man was the best. He taught Sam the skills for staying alive because every job had a different outcome. He prayed this one had a happy ending for Alena's sake.

Oh, hell. Nothing explained why the boss' daughter had grated on his nerves. Maybe because he hadn't been laid for a while. A good possibility and one that was his own fault. He had a willing woman pushing him into the shadows by the pool. Hell, they could have done it in the pool house changing room. Bing, bang, boom. Thank you, ma'am.

But he couldn't do it. He hated the one-night

stands. They meant nothing except a satisfaction of animal urge. Besides, the woman should put herself on a pedestal since he was half-afraid something would break if he touched her. The boss had money. The daughter spent it. A man had to have a screw loose to hook up with a woman like that. And desperate. Sam McCullen wasn't desperate.

Why did he even go? It was a party full of glitz and glam. Sparkling crystal, bubbling champagne, stodgy music. The kind of party where he forced his eyes to stay open, pretending to listen to people who were boring as hell. He didn't have to go. The boss knew his real purpose at the bank.

Unless he wanted Sam to hook up with the daughter.

Now, that made sense. The woman had zeroed in as soon as Sam stepped through the door. She rubbed against him in ways no decent woman should. Didn't do a thing for him. No arousal. No tingling. Just an itch that he couldn't scratch. She had the audacity to ask if he was gay when he refused an outright proposition. He used his injury as an excuse. Thank God for the cast. It gave him the graceful out he needed.

Almost. He had contemplated taking her on to get her off his back, but a condom required the use of two hands. He'd ask her to do it, but dear Lord, the nails on her fingers! If she so much as slipped, he'd be singing soprano.

No, the cast was his godsend. A man required the use of two hands to send a woman into ecstasy.

His excuse anyway.

Unfortunately, he refused a willing woman for one who was not.

He should have his head examined.

Alena said she would wait up. That didn't mean she wouldn't fall asleep on the sofa. What did her fiancé do to force such a beautiful woman to spend every night alone? It wasn't healthy. Nor explainable. She had a stroke, and he left. It had filled her with abandonment issues. Certainly a feeling of false love. But there was more to the story. Somehow, someway, he needed to get her to talk.

Sam undid his bowtie. Either he stood here all night looking like a lost fool, or he approached the one woman who intrigued him, who had the answers that brought him east.

A movement caught his eye. He froze, senses on full alert. *Well, I'll be damned.* Someone lurked in the shadows of the evergreen by her door.

Unacceptable. Who the hell wasn't doing their job?

Sam approached her apartment lifting a hand poised to knock. With a quick sidestep, his fist swung down and connected with a crack to a man's face. The body slid against the brick wall in a slump.

It wasn't the man from the park. This body was bigger with a little more meat on his bones.

Sam took out his cell phone and typed a text message. *Send a car. NOW. Her place.*

Several minutes later, a black sedan with tinted windows pulled up. A back door swung open. Sam grabbed the man by the collar and with one swift maneuver, tossed him into the back seat.

"Someone was supposed to be watching," he said into the black interior. "Where the hell is he?"

"I'll find out," said a voice.

"What about the rear?"

"I'll check and get back to you."

The door closed as quietly as it opened. The car drove off.

Sam fumed. Alena was never to be left unguarded. He was so mad at the security breach he could chew on a brick.

Calm down. He didn't get in.

She was vulnerable. All it took was an inattentive moment, and she would disappear. Then what would they do? What if he spent the night with the boss' daughter? Didn't anyone do their job right?

After several long minutes to control his anger, Sam rapped on her door. She answered a few seconds later wide-awake and perky.

"Did you make a noise?" she asked. "I thought I heard something."

"Yeah, you heard a drunk stumbling on the pavement. He went into one of the apartments on the end."

She hurried him in and shut the door. "The guide's about to be eaten by beetles!" she said. She pointed to the TV. "I'm watching *The Mummy* on late night. Oh, yuk, there he goes. Gross." She curled up on the sofa.

His anger dissipated into a puff of smoke. This was why he gave up a night with the boss' daughter. Alena made him feel good, as simple as that. He liked the sound of her voice, the wave of her hair, and he absolutely adored her silk pajamas. Still no robe. What a treat! The silk stimulated her nipples. He had seen it earlier. He saw it now. That did more for him than any woman rubbing his private parts.

He threw his suit jacket on a chair, stuffed his loosened tie into his pocket, and then sat on the sofa with her. He grabbed a large handful of popcorn. "You won't be able to sleep after a movie like this," he said.

"Sure I will. My dad and I watched all the scary movies together while my mom hid in the bedroom. There's beer in the fridge if you want it."

He did want it. The champagne at the party was godawful stuff. Bitter as hell. Nothing cold and refreshing like a beer. Sam grabbed one for Alena while he was at it. At the commercial break, he said, "Undo my cummerbund, beautiful. I feel like I'm wearing a girdle."

"It is a girdle," she said matter-of-factly. "It was invented by some fat man who needed to hide his big belly." She undid it.

"You made that up!"

She sat back with a grin. "It makes sense. Women wear girdles. Some women," she corrected.

He whooshed out a large puff of air. "I can breathe again!" He stuck out his arm. "Here. Undo the cufflink while you're undressing me."

My God, she blushed! She tried to conceal it by shoving the cufflink into his hand before grabbing hold of her beer, but even her ears turned red. So cute. He smiled at her. "That blush put a lot of color in your cheeks."

"Don't get any ideas. It's from the beer." She took a swig. "You're going to have a nasty bruise on that right knuckle soon. What did you hit this time?"

He looked at it. The guy's nose might need some plastic surgery. "It isn't easy doing everything with one hand," he explained. "I guess I thumped it on something."

"Well, don't come pleading for my help if we have

47

to put that hand in a cast, too." She chuckled.

"Your mind is in the gutter."

"Yes, it is and an amusing one at that." She looked at him. "I take it you didn't get lucky tonight."

"Actually, I did, but I turned her down."

"Liar."

"She was the boss' daughter, Alena. She had too much to drink and was falling all over me. I won't take advantage of a woman that way."

"I knew there was a reason I liked you." She said it with affection, which surprised him. He wanted to believe he heard more in her tone, but he should get his ears checked to prove it.

She gave him a long look. "Are you sure she won't use that against you? A vendetta kind of thing? Woman scorned, all that? How'd you get out of it?"

He held up his cast.

"Smart move," she said. "What about the next time?"

"There won't be a next time. I'll take a bodyguard, namely you."

She laughed and took another swig of her beer.

While she watched the movie, he watched her. Comparing Alena Nichols to the boss' daughter was a no-brainer. Sam had seen enough of the plastic surgery types in LA, but Alena was real. He liked what he saw: a woman without make-up, relaxed and curled up at the other end of the sofa, seductive without knowing it. In his mind, a woman who tested his self-control. He almost didn't go to the party tonight, but everything worked out better than he expected. He smiled to himself at the thought.

When he could take his gaze off her, he looked

around her apartment. The layout was the same for every apartment in the complex: small kitchen with a counter and stools, blending into a nice size living room, one bedroom and bath. Family photos hung on the wall. Her mom and dad more likely. She and Nan Bauer dressed in cap and gown. No fiancé, of course. Understandable.

In a corner display, she had an array of miniature Victorian houses on a three-tiered stand. Some were lit like a Christmas tree. "You collect those?" he asked.

"Yes. I started after my stroke. When I get a chance, I go to flea markets, which isn't often. Wow, look at that dust cloud! It's amazing what they do with special effects these days. You know—" She pointed her beer bottle at the TV. "That mummy guy isn't bad-looking."

"You're drunk."

Her mouth fell open. "I am not!"

"Sure you are. You're ogling a mummy on TV when you have a good-looking stud sitting right next to you."

"Oh." She snickered. "Sorry." She laughed aloud. The sound was music to his ears.

"I ate all your popcorn," he said.

She looked at the empty bowl. "I can make more."

"Not for me. I've eaten too much tonight." Her eyes glowed. The color of sunshine on desert sand. Maybe she really was drunk. "You know, Alena, I'm a little disappointed in you."

She stared. "Why?"

"Most women shriek at a scary movie. Then they bury their face against a guy's chest. You're never going to do that with me."

49

She smiled at her bottle. "Probably not."

"Is that why you became a doctor because you handle scary stuff?"

"It might have something to do with it. Nan Bauer and I worked together in the ER for years, and we saw our fair share of blood and guts. It never bothered me. After my stroke, I transferred to radiology because the ER pace was too exhausting. I still cover for someone every now and then. It helps keep my skills up." She shifted to face him. "I often wonder about fate."

"How so?"

"Johnny bobbed into the ER one day on a consult call, and Cupid hit. Classic love at first sight. Shows you how wrong that was."

"Johnny, your fiancé? I felt the same about Christine, my ex-wife. Despite what she did to me, I still believe in love at first sight. Tell me about Johnny."

"I'd rather not."

All right. He took a shot and lost.

Alena shook herself and smiled. "Your obvious proposition aside, did you have a good time at the party?"

"No. Stuffed shirts surrounded me. I should have asked you to come."

"Then the boss' daughter would never have flirted. Going stag was a good idea. It gave all the women a chance to assess you."

He frowned while fussing with the crease on his pant leg. "You make me sound like a piece of meat."

"You might get a lot more offers at the next party, and you should accept one. Dating will force you to discover the city and surrounding areas. For the record,

I'd have turned you down. I don't own a gown." She paused with her gaze glued to the TV. "Uh-oh, this guy's gonna get eaten by beetles, too. Yuk! In the dark even. Oh, dear!" She cringed when the man screamed. "I'm sorry I missed this in the theater."

"It came out years ago. You were still in a cradle."

"I wish." She put her head back on the sofa cushion.

Sleep clouded the desert sand. The beer and late night had kicked in, but he wanted to push his luck a bit further.

"Your fiancé must be a real jerk if he left a beautiful woman like you."

Her mouth lifted at the corners. He could see she was pleased.

"That was a nice thing to say, Sam."

"I meant every word. Was he from around here?"

She shook her head. "Ohio. It's possible he went back there and stayed away from his father."

"But you don't know for sure."

"He could be anywhere. Don't know, don't care." She lifted her head. "You want to beat him up for me?"

"If you tell me where he is, sure." He held up his right hand and made a fist. "I think I can do it one-handed."

She put her head back onto the cushion. "I've learned that life can be cruel, Sam. Not only did Johnny leave me at a critical time, but after my parents put my furniture in storage, someone broke in and trashed everything."

His head snapped. "They did?"

"Actually, not *they*. One lone woman broke into the storage area. She ripped everything to shreds. She busted the lamps and dumped every drawer. My mom and dad handled the mess. I was still in rehab."

"Anything missing?"

"Nothing valuable was stored there. The police thought she was looking for something specific. It was also possible she broke into the wrong unit." She yawned. "They never found out who she was. She hid her face from the security cameras, but it was definitely a woman. Black wig, loose black clothing. She wore gloves so no prints."

A pro, he mused. An unexpected piece of news. He watched her. "How about your office?"

"I didn't have one, but now that you mentioned it, someone did break into my locker in the ER doctor's lounge. And to top everything off, someone stole my car. The police found it stripped."

"Wow. It does sound as if someone was looking for something. What could it be?"

"I think it was bad luck. This is Philadelphia, Sammie."

"That guy on the park bench wanted something."

She lifted her head. "I hadn't thought of that."

As much as he wanted to know more, there would come another time. He stood to his feet.

"I guess I'm about as undressed as I can be with you. I enjoyed the beer and popcorn more than my entire evening at the party."

"I'm not pushing you out."

"I know, but you're sleepy. I don't want to end my night carrying this sleepy woman to her bed when she looks so sexy in her silk pajamas."

The blush returned, deeper, redder, and hotter. "Oh, God!" She grabbed a magazine to fan herself.

"I'm so sorry, Sam. It felt too warm to put on a robe. I wasn't thinking."

He thought all night, of her in bed, of her naked, of every possible maneuver they could do together. She stood to her feet and walked him to the door. In bare feet, she looked fragile. He smiled at her.

"I'm glad I got you for a friend, Alena. I would have preferred watching the whole movie with you rather than attend a boring anniversary party." He bent down and kissed her cheek. She smelled of beer, popcorn, and...flowers. A face full of uncertainty stared back at him. He would break that uncertainty one day. It could take time. It should take patience, but this beautiful doctor was going to be his. Sam smiled to himself as he walked out the door.

His cell phone chirped halfway across the parking lot. Another text message. *Re pkg found. JG confirmed. Use caution.*

He cursed and continued toward his apartment. He no sooner closed the door and turned on a light when a second message came through. *Asleep on the job. Drinking. Ass fired. New man in position. Rear was covered.*

It couldn't kill the anger boiling in his gut. He heaved the phone onto the kitchen counter.

Chapter Seven

Alena loved this sidewalk café. She loved sitting at one of the small tables under an open sky to watch the world pass by. Cars, people, even the occasional smoke-spewing bus; it didn't matter. It made her feel like part of the living again. She especially loved sharing it with Nan, a rare treat these days. Top it with a decent glass of wine, an exceptional meal, and life couldn't be better.

Unfortunately, Nan had a ferocious appetite. The table was never big enough. The waiter earned his keep as he whisked one plate away to replace it with another. They sat tucked in the far corner by the wrought-iron fence.

"I wish you'd stop laughing, Alena. You're creating a scene."

"I can't help it. Every time I think about him, I laugh. He looked so cute standing there helpless."

"Cute! The guy's a behemoth!"

Alena smiled and swirled her wine. "You had to be there." She was glad Nan wasn't. Sam's light kiss on her cheek had activated a lot of buried sensations. A strong sense of trust for one.

Nan sat back in her chair to study her friend. "I'm seeing a little more of the old Alena Nichols over here. Sam is the cause."

Alena gazed into her wine glass. "Maybe."

"A definite maybe, dear. Why else would you sit here laughing your head off? It's not like you undid his belt and dropped his pants. Big deal, a cufflink and a cummerbund." Then quickly, "Did you want to?"

"What, drop his pants?" The urge had crossed her mind once or twice, however fleeting, but memories had flooded in, memories that were painful. As hard as she tried, she couldn't dismiss them. Two years had passed, and the memories were as vivid as yesterday. She gulped the last of her wine. "You know me better than that."

"Yes, I do, but I'm forever optimistic. I haven't seen you laugh like this in years. Sam has a wonderful affect on you."

"Don't get your hopes up. We're friends. We have every intention of keeping it that way."

"Uh-huh." She buttered the last piece of bread. "He's not a bad-looking guy to end your dry spell."

Alena made a face. "He went through a nasty divorce. He's not interested. And neither am I." She signaled for the waiter. "Can we have some coffee please?"

Nan finished her bread then foraged for more. She found a lone breadstick hiding near her napkin. The woman had emptied the breadbasket, finished a large salad, a cup of soup plus an entrée with two sides. She hadn't said anything about dessert yet. She must be sick.

"I think Sam's a fine specimen to get your juices going," Nan said. "You should give him a try. I'm sure he'll accommodate you if you ask."

"That would change a platonic relationship into one neither of us want."

"Yeah, but a platonic relationship between a man and a woman has a tendency to fail. Hormones take over."

"I'll keep that in mind."

Nan reached across the table and took Alena's hand. "I'd like to erase your fear. I'd like to send you back in time to when you were carefree and pretty, when you were willing to fall in love. But I can't. You are still pretty so all we need is to get back your carefree spirit. Then you won't be afraid to fall in love again. Sam is breaking through, and that's a start." She squeezed Alena's hand with affection before releasing it as the waiter returned with their coffee. Alena reached for the cream; Nan grabbed the sugar.

Alena kept quiet about Sam stirring up her juices that night. He had looked gorgeous in his tuxedo. Couple that with his gravelly voice tingling her nerve endings along with hazel eyes that pierced through her pajamas, hell, yeah, she was a trifle turned on. Her hormones did jumping jacks inside her. She ran straight into the shower after he left.

She'd dreamt of him all night. She tossed and turned while struggling to push him out of her mind. She wasn't ready for him. Not yet. Too many friggin' hang-ups caused by a fiancé who didn't give a horse's ass about her.

She had often wondered what life would be like if her stroke never happened. What if she had married Johnny and then had a stroke? Would he have disappeared and stuck her with that big Victorian house? What if they had kids?

You can't predict the future.

True, but she didn't want to repeat the past either.

The present could be controlled, and she intended to maintain that control. A platonic relationship was the best way.

While she sipped her coffee, her gaze drifted to the crowded bar visible through a set of wide-open double doors. A man sat alone drinking Perrier on the rocks while reading a newspaper.

"Nice looking guy," Nan said, following her gaze. "I've seen him before."

Alena looked at her. "Where?"

"At the hospital. Hanging around. Mostly the lobby. He's got the most attractive head of salt and pepper hair. It makes you want to run your fingers through it."

Alena agreed. The man looked to be in his forties with muscled arms holding his newspaper. She caught Nan salivating.

"How'd you like that hunk sitting at your breakfast table every morning?" Nan asked.

"Do you know who he is?"

"No, but he must have family admitted on one of the floors. I've seen him for several weeks now. See how much you miss by hiding in that dark reading room?"

Alena threw the empty breadbasket at her. "I pass through the lobby every morning and evening to get to the garage. I never see him."

"He's there during the day. Usually sitting in a chair reading the newspaper. Like now."

The coffee tasted a tad burnt tonight. She loaded it with more cream. "The ER is a far cry from the lobby, Nan. Are you flirting with him?"

Nan's mouth fell open, aghast. "Of course not!"

She tilted her head. "The snack shop is in the lobby. I get hungry."

It should have been Alena's first clue, but Nan had a reputation with men. She was a feisty little devil in bed. Her calendar was full with appointments both for day and night.

Something behind Alena caught Nan's attention. Her sharp eyes locked onto it like a hawk sighting its next meal. Alena understood her friend well enough to wait before turning. More than once, she'd found herself face-to-face with the object of Nan's scrutinizing stare.

After several long seconds, Nan leaned forward on the table. In a low voice, she said, "Check out the two Neanderthals coming our way. One of them is yours."

Surprised, Alena turned to see Sam and a black man walking toward the café. They were equal in size and stature, both oblivious of the passersby who moved out of their way.

"They look like two linebackers plowing down the sidewalk," Alena said. "Between two sets of broad shoulders and streetlights, the pavement isn't wide enough for a person to get around them."

"Who's the black guy?"

"I've no idea."

They were having an animated discussion with hand gestures mimicking ball throwing. Sports, she guessed. Man talk. No wonder they were oblivious.

"I think they came out of the fitness club across the street," Nan said. "They might be heading for the bar inside." She grunted as she watched them. "Neanderthals in nice clothes." Nan's gaze stripped them naked. Something pleased her. Alena recognized the look that flashed onto her face, and it meant trouble.

"We already know Sam is a bank president," Nan said in a low voice. "The other guy could be a bouncer at a strip joint or maybe he works at the fitness club. Gad, look at the size of him! Want me to call them over?"

"Wait!"

Too late. Impulse Nan already caught Sam's attention and waved. The two men made their way through the crowded table area looking like two bullies with big smiles on their faces.

"Now, this is what I call a good day," Sam said as they approached. "Dr. Alena Nichols, Dr. Nan Bauer, meet Nathan Donagher. We play racquetball together."

"You're a good match," Nan blurted.

Nan was a little obvious with her scrutiny of Nathan Donagher. He, like Sam, had a linebacker build with a muscled chest and thick arms. Also like Sam, he was handsome in his own way with a nose slightly askew and a scar that split one eyebrow in two. His most dominant feature was a bald head that glistened under the café lights. He wasn't good-looking to make women melt when he passed, but he wasn't bad-looking either. Like Sam.

Shit. She should stop comparing.

"We only popped in for a beer," Sam said.

"Speak for yourself, Blondie. I can always eat." Nathan grabbed an empty chair and sat alongside Nan. His dark eyes glowed as he scanned her with equal scrutiny.

The man had a deep basilar tone to his voice that resonated from within his chest. A man's voice. Like Sam's gravelly tone, the kind that groaned with sexual pleasure in a woman's ear.

She should have refused that second glass of wine.

Sam followed Nathan's maneuver and placed a chair next to Alena. "You ladies aren't finished, I hope."

"I could go for some dessert," Nan said without taking her gaze off Nathan.

Nathan's brows shot up in surprise. "Chocolate or vanilla?"

"Oh, definitely chocolate," she answered. "Maybe with a touch of whipped cream."

Alena groaned.

Sam nudged her arm. "There's a lot of heat coming from the other side of the table. Maybe you and I should go into the bar and leave them alone."

This was a common occurrence where Nan was involved. She was unpredictable and impulsive and attracted men because of it. More than once, Alena had turned into the third wheel with retreat as her only option.

Not tonight, however. She leaned forward on the table. "I need to remind Nan that she is due in at work in thirty minutes." She glared at her friend.

"I can do a lot in a half hour," Nan said in a low sultry voice. Then she forced her attention away from Nathan and sighed. "Yes, all right. Alena is reminding me of my responsible self. I didn't sit here nursing a half glass of wine for nothing."

"Aw, give us at least five minutes," Sam pleaded. "You have a ten minute walk to the hospital. It's not far." He nudged Nathan's arm. "She's good with hands." He held up his cast.

"Is she now?" A wide grin spread onto his lips.

His tone was sexual in nature, deep and seductive. It had a way of tingling a woman's nerves, a good tingle. Alena expected Nan to jump him right there on the table.

"Five minutes will lead to ten," Nan said, "and then I'll have to run to the hospital and leave Alena behind." She pushed her chair away.

Nathan stopped her from rising. "Is Nan a middle name?"

"It's a first name, short for Nanette."

"What the hell kind of name is Nanette for a black woman?"

"About as common as Nathan for a black man. I like it."

"What, Nathan?"

"No, Nanette. I'm named after my grandmother." She grabbed her purse. "You guys can have our table if you want."

"Not if you're leaving," Sam said. "Nate and I can sit at the bar."

"Yeah," Nathan growled. "Two men sitting at a sidewalk table start rumors that lead to fights. I'm too old for that stuff."

"Then I guess you shave your head to hide the gray," Nan blurted. "Very clever."

Alena dropped her chin to her chest with a groan.

Sam slapped Nathan on his broad back. "The woman saw right through you, old man."

"What the hell does she know? She's a little squirt who got her doctor degree from a cereal box."

"Squirt!" Nan's nostrils flared.

Oops! Nan's sensitivity to her height raised her temper faster than any comment about her medical degree. Nathan was about to discover that this little squirt had the compact body of a wolverine and could damn near fight like one.

Alena jumped to her feet and grabbed her friend before Nan thumped the man. "Come on. Let's pay the bill and get out of here. Gentlemen, have a pleasant meal. Nice to meet you, Mr. Donagher."

Alena forced the wolverine through the crowded café. Like dragging a child throwing a tantrum. However, she knew her friend well, and that meant getting her out and away from her target.

When they walked halfway down the block, Nan turned to her. "Do me a favor. After you pick up your car from the garage, go back there and run over Nathan for me."

Alena shuddered. "I've never seen heat turn to ice so fast. You were about to cause a scene. I don't think the hospital would appreciate seeing one of their popular doctors in the news."

Nan grunted in answer. "I'm not a little squirt." She pouted.

"No, you're not, and you shouldn't be so sensitive about it. He was teasing you. Compared to those two guys, we're both little squirts." She hooked her arm through Nan's. "I think Nathan likes you."

"Ha! Fat chance on him seeing me again. He's not in my league."

An odd statement coming from Nan Bauer. Most men were in her league as long as they could function, in particular, satisfy.

As they approached the hospital, Alena released Nan's arm. "Are you calmed down yet?"

Nan grunted in answer. Then, a wry grin twisted

her lips. "He was kinda cute."

"I thought so."

Nan hugged Alena and entered the hospital. Alena continued toward the parking garage and burst out laughing. She continued to laugh all the way to her car.

A stupid mistake. She dropped her guard, and no one dropped their guard in Philadelphia especially in a parking garage.

A man approached from behind her vehicle. He wore black with a hoodie covering most of his face, but she recognized the body. He was the weasel from the park bench. The hairs stood up on the back of her neck. *Uh, oh.*

"I want your purse, lady." He waved a knife.

What a sitting duck! She couldn't run because of her leg. She could waffle him with the cane, but then what?

She pressed the panic button on her car remote. The blare echoed off the garage walls, deafening both of them.

Out of nowhere, a man approached. He grabbed the knife, threw a solid fist into the mugger's nose, and kneed him in the gut. The mugger dropped to the ground with a groan.

Her rescuer was the salt and pepper haired man!

"I saw you at the café!" Alena said with surprise.

"Yeah, I saw you, too. Can you cut the noise?" He nodded toward the car. "Wow, nice and loud. Are you all right?"

She nodded. "Just a little shook up." It unnerved her to see the weasel man. He *had* to be the one following her all these weeks. Why, dammit? What did she have that he wanted?

"If the hospital put the extra cameras out here instead of my office, we wouldn't have this problem," she complained. "I noticed security didn't come running. I'll call them now." She took out her phone.

"No, wait a minute. What are you talking about 'cameras in your office'?"

"I had it removed. The garage could use a few more angled cameras instead. It would make the area safer."

"I'll agree with that, but someone has to sit and watch the monitor to be effective." He grabbed the mugger by the collar. "I'll take him to security. I want to talk to them because I'm coming here a lot. This shouldn't happen." He hauled the man to his feet.

"I'm bleeding!" the weasel complained. "You broke my nose!"

"Consider yourself lucky you're still alive," he said. To Alena, "I'm Dave by the way."

"Thank you, Dave. I can go to security with you."

"No, get yourself home. I'll take care of this guy."

He walked off, dragging the bleeding mugger with him.

Before her stroke, her foot would have connected to the man's balls without a second of hesitation. Then, she'd run like hell before he recovered. The stroke had changed everything in her life including her vulnerability. It depressed her to think she didn't have the guts to fight anymore.

No, that wasn't the right mindset. She would fight like hell if necessary. Alena still had usable arms and legs. But to run? How would she know if she could or could not run? She never tried.

She hurried into her car and locked the doors.

Chapter Eight

Alena's nerves were frazzled. Twice, this weasel man had entered her life. Why? What did he want? *Be specific, dammit.* Like whoever had ripped her apartment furnishings to shreds or stripped her car. What were they looking for?

She had no answers. Best to let it go, chalk it up as another mounting mystery surrounding her life.

The following Saturday was a perfect day for cleaning but as usual, the morning started off with a bang. First, the sweeper hose broke into two parts from dry rot. It took forever to find the duct tape. Alena should have listened to her inner voice and bought a new one instead of taking her mother's leftover. Then the coffeemaker exploded on the kitchen counter. What a mess. Coffee and glass everywhere. It took forever to clean it up. One mishap after another. Now, the doorbell. She couldn't be madder at the interruption. She threw the door open with more force than she intended.

Sam stood there. His hazel eyes grew wide as his hands flew up in defense. "Whoa! You're not gonna use that on me, are you?"

Surprised, Alena followed his pointing finger to the wrench in her hand. "Sorry. I'm in the middle of fixing my toilet."

"What's wrong with the toilet?"

"The little thingy in the tank came undone."

He took the wrench from her hand. "Let me see."

Alena led him to the bathroom. Sam saw the problem and reached in. "You don't need a wrench for this, honey. It's a hand-tightening nut."

She looked around him since it was impossible to see over his shoulder. "I'm a doctor, not a plumber. Can you fix it?"

"It's already fixed." He flushed the toilet and replaced the tank lid. "How about I take you out?"

"I'm not dressed to go out." She wore a tee-shirt and sweatpants, both two sizes too big.

"You'd look good in rags."

"These *are* rags. They're perfect for cleaning, which is what I'm trying to do, but everything in the place is breaking on me. I'm having a hell of a time getting anything done."

"Then it's perfect timing on my part. Give it up and take a ride with me."

A tempting offer. She eyed him from head to toe. "Where did you want to go?"

"How about the river? I heard there are sculler races today." He spotted the sweeper in the hall. "Maybe you'd like to do some shopping. It looks like you could use a new vacuum cleaner."

She had made a mess with the duct tape. If she wrapped a leg wound like that, they would kick her out of the hospital. "Buying a woman a vacuum cleaner is not a short cut to her heart, Sam McCullen. Besides, I can afford my own. I'll buy it the next time I feel like shopping." She ushered him out of the bathroom toward the living room. She should push him right out the door and get on with cleaning, but something held her back.

His aftershave for one. His company for another. She liked having him around.

Or maybe she wanted an excuse to skip cleaning day.

He turned to face her. "Let's go to the river, Alena. It might be fun. Humor me."

"My funny bone went down the toilet with that flush." The man was too damn nice for such snappy words. "Look, Sam. You can't expect me to be cheery because you showed up. This is my cleaning day."

"Do it later. It's too beautiful to spend the day indoors."

She had ignored that bright observation ever since she opened her eyes and looked out the window. It took all her determination to put on rags and start cleaning.

Yeah, you accomplished so much, too.

Well, the kitchen was spotless.

"All right, it sounds like fun, but only if we stop at the store on the way home. I need a new coffeemaker." She headed for the bedroom.

"It's a deal. Where you going?"

"I'm changing first." No way in hell would she go out the door in these rags.

Soft jazz flowed through the stereo speakers as he drove. He kept the volume low, a barely audible, seductive tone that relaxed her frayed nerves. The music combined with the soft leather seats, hell, it was better than a soak in a tub. She hoped he took a trip to Jersey and back.

Neither of them talked. From time to time, she glanced his way to see him doing the same to her. After thirty minutes of driving, she wondered if they really were heading to Jersey. "What river?" she asked.

"Schuylkill." He cocked his head. "It's a beautiful day for a picnic, don't you think?"

"A picnic?" Alena perked up. "That's a wonderful idea. I haven't been on a picnic in years. What about food?"

"Everything's in the trunk. I thought it might be fun to watch the races and eat at the same time."

They chatted away from that point, commenting on whatever struck them. A passersby, a woman's clothes, a man on a bicycle. Throughout, she couldn't help taking a glance into the door's side view mirror. A gray car followed at a distance, had been for several miles. Two male occupants occupied the front seat.

"I think I'm paranoid. Correct me if I'm wrong, but we're being followed."

Sam checked his rearview mirror. "The gray car? Yeah, I noticed them. It could be a coincidence."

"I don't believe in coincidences anymore, Sam. Too much is happening to me."

"All right, then. Let's see if they follow."

He turned a corner. He turned another corner. The car followed.

"You've done this before," she said.

"The question is what to do about it now. Is there something you're not telling me?"

Her head snapped. "You think they're following *me*?"

"Well, it can't be me. The guy on the park bench started it. You said he wanted something. What was it?"

"For your information, that guy attempted to mug me in the parking garage at the hospital. A nice man beat him up and hauled him to security. So, it can't be him behind us."

He almost slammed the car into a line of parked cars. He jerked the steering wheel. "Why didn't you tell me this earlier?"

"Sorry. I didn't know I was supposed to fill you in." He sounded awful possessive all of a sudden. It made her uneasy.

Sam grit his teeth. "My mistake. Our friendship doesn't have a whole lot of ground rules, but you're turning into my best friend. I don't want you to get hurt."

Best friend? Well, okay, yeah. A possibility she never considered. "What now?"

He glanced into the rearview mirror. "Let's see if we can lose these guys. We'll figure out what they want later."

He turned a corner, another corner. The car followed. One last corner. They watched the gray car go straight.

"I think they figured out what we were doing," she said.

"Good because I want to enjoy my time with you today. Let's turn a few more corners to be sure."

After several miles and no gray car, they relaxed as the river came into view. Sam parked the car and then led her to a grassy knoll not far from a busy runner's path. The setting was perfect. The river flowed before them, the runner's path behind. The setting offered some privacy but not enough to make her feel isolated.

Sam spread out a blanket and arranged an array of goodies from a large basket. He even took out linen napkins and china. The coffee he poured from a large flask, piping hot and delicious. She sampled everything and felt very much like a kid in a candy shop.

This was much better than cleaning. She took a bite of a blueberry muffin. Her eyes rolled. "Oh, yum! Try one of these. It melts in your mouth." She looked at him. He had a silly grin on his face. "You can't tell me a hunky guy like you has a picnic basket stuffed in a closet."

"No. There's a deli I go to near the fitness club. I told the owner I wanted to take a beautiful woman on a picnic. He packed everything you see here. Try the little bagels. They're my favorite." He popped one into his mouth.

After all the sampling and not a scrap left, they rested on the blanket propped up with pillows, cups of coffee in their hands, watching the races.

"Why aren't you dating some rich doctor?" he asked after a time.

"I haven't dated anyone, Sam, let alone another doctor." She picked some crumbs off the blanket and tossed them into the grass. She was slow and deliberate about it, too. "Need I remind you I was engaged to one?"

"Rich?"

"Well, no. Comfortable would be the word. He worked in a busy practice."

"If he—"

She touched his arm to stop him. "Talking about Johnny is very painful, Sam. Please don't."

He nodded. "I'll change the subject. You don't wear any jewelry."

He changed the subject all right. "Neither do you."

"I'm too big for jewelry. I look like a Christmas tree. What's your excuse?"

"I only wear a watch when I work."

He lifted her chin. "Pearls would fit you well."

"Don't get any ideas, Mr. McCullen."

This had to stop. She gulped the last of her coffee. "We better go. I need that coffeemaker."

They packed everything into the basket and shook out the blanket. She had the urge to run toward the car, but he grabbed her hand and held her back. They strolled instead. She looked at him.

"I made an interesting discovery about male doctors," she said. "They tend to be a little too self-absorbed. I like normal conversations."

"Like ours?"

"Yeah, like ours." She hid a smile. "I wanted you to know that." Why, she had no clue. Because he was nice. Because he got under her skin. Because he was one man who might stick around.

"Sam?"

He looked at her, one brow raised in question.

"Thank you for a lovely afternoon."

He threw the basket and blanket into the trunk and slammed it. He wrapped his arms around her before she had a chance to move toward the front of the car. He lifted her chin. "Because I want to," he said and kissed her hard.

The maneuver surprised her.

What surprised her more, she didn't pull away. She sucked in the taste of his lips with a greed that boiled from deep within her gut. When he lifted his head, his gaze sparkled.

"This is not how to maintain a platonic relationship," she mused.

"Maybe I'd like to change the rules. Are you game?"

She broke free of his arms. "It's a little early for me. I'd like to keep things as they are. Please don't be mad."

He took her hand and guided her toward the front of the car. "I could never be mad at you, Alena." He opened the door. "Let's get you that coffeemaker."

Chapter Nine

Sam sat in a corner booth sipping coffee while watching the lunch crowd gather. It was a busy little restaurant. Three servers ran around taking orders and delivering food, balancing overloaded trays with skill. The boss said to eat. So, he ate. Roast beef on rye.

The man he waited for strolled through the door and looked around. Mike Donovan had a distinguished way about him. A man who had money and spent it. Well-made clothes to fit a tall frame, perfectly trimmed hair, manicured nails. Not a man who got his hands dirty. Sam gestured to get his attention.

The text message he had received this morning sounded urgent. For Donovan to request a meeting before the completion of the job, hell, yeah, something was wrong. There were already too many surprises with this assignment. He had a strange feeling Donovan was about to present him with a whopper.

Donovan sat in the booth opposite and ordered a coffee with a piece of apple pie. "We have a problem." He paused as the server placed the pie and coffee before him. When she moved on, he took a photo from his suit jacket. He handed it to Sam.

The photo was of a woman taken by a surveillance camera inside his bank. Sam recognized the wild-haired mane of blond hair. "When was this taken?"

"Yesterday. She drove here from LA. We don't

know how long she's been watching you. Did she go to your office?"

"I wasn't in the office yesterday."

"It's your ex, correct?"

"Yes, it's Christine." She looked like a hag in the photo. Too much meth, crack, booze. All of the above.

"I want to know how she found you," Donovan asked.

He'd like to know that as well. "I haven't seen her since our divorce."

"Your family back in LA perhaps?"

Sam shook his head. "They have no idea where I am. They reach me by cell phone."

Donovan took a bite of his pie before continuing. "She's going to compromise this entire operation, McCullen. She's well aware of what you do for a living, and I know damn well she isn't here to say hello."

"No. She's here to cause trouble." He stared at the photo. She used to be so pretty. Now, she looked like a truck dragged her under its wheels. "I can't believe how she's changed." Just staring at the photo rattled him. She came so close. What if he was with Alena? Months of work down the toilet. "Christine knows how I work and who I work with. Someone talked."

"Yes. I'll handle that end. *You* have to handle your ex." Donovan took out a piece of paper and slid it across the table. "She's staying at a hotel six blocks from the bank. It will be a matter of time before she shows up at your apartment. I don't want that to happen. Do I make myself clear, McCullen?"

Sam agreed. "I'll take care of her." He didn't know how yet. She was here because she didn't give a shit about endangering his life. She knew the dangers in his job. He'd made many enemies over the years, people who would love to put a bullet in him, and Christine was one of them. "I'll take care of her," he told Donovan.

****

Sam stood outside the hotel door checking for the fourth time the room number. It was a roach-infested establishment, the type of place where one booked by the hour. Even as he paced the hall, customers came and went. No bed sheets were changed, if there were bed sheets at all. It took too much time.

He didn't want to do this. He had paced the hall for ten minutes unwilling to confront the woman who still tore at his heart. He, Sam McCullen, a trained professional, was afraid to confront the devil behind the door. What if she refused to listen? What would he do then?

She had become a monster on meth. She stalked and hounded until he realized his hands reached for her throat. He mustn't let her jeopardize this job. He *had* to do something.

He took a deep breath and knocked.

The door flew open to reveal the woman who was once a prom queen. Her blonde hair was stringy with oil, her once-beautiful eyes sunk halfway into her skull. Her creamy skin had changed into pockmarks and scabs as if she had a chronic case of shingles.

"I figured you'd show up," Christine taunted.

She always had a way of grating his nerves. She also knew how to catch his attention.

"Standing in the middle of the bank lobby wasn't a bright idea." He stepped in. The door swung shut behind him with a bang.

"I did that on purpose. I know how you guys work."

She knew too much, and that made her dangerous. "Why are you here?"

"You know why. I want to expose you so that someone can put a bullet in you once and for all."

Donovan was right. Christine would blow the job wide open. She had become vindictive and unpredictable, a fatal combination brought on by drugs frying her brain. Her quest for revenge could get several people killed...including Alena.

"Who told you where I was?" he asked.

She grinned, showing a mouth full of rotted teeth. "I still have friends."

Yeah, friends who put his life in jeopardy.

"If I die, Christine, that stops your alimony payments. Where will you get your drug money?"

"Ha! Like you're giving me enough to keep me comfortable. I can earn money without you, bastard."

"Selling your body isn't the answer." Visions of STD combined with HIV made him cringe. Who the hell would sleep with such a hag?

Another druggie, of course.

As he stepped further into the room, the sight on the table by the window stopped him. Drug paraphernalia covered the table along with a half-eaten burger and several condom packets. The needle and metal spoon bothered him most. No weapons that he could see. The bed looked as if it hadn't been made in days. Her wastebasket overflowed with fast food containers with a cockroach having a field day. And were there bedbugs on the sheets?

Shit, head lice.

"Doesn't this hotel have housekeeping?" he asked with disgust.

"I ain't letting no stranger in here."

A stranger could report her to the police, her biggest fear. A third strike would put her in the can for a while.

"I see you graduated to heroin," he said.

"Easier to get."

Reality was a harsh pill. She was right.

"You need to return to LA, Christine. You can't stay."

"Not until I hear someone put a bullet in you. Then I can go with a smile on my face. You got any cigarettes?"

"You know I don't smoke."

"Yeah, I guess it depends on what role you're playing. A bank president of all things. What a joke." She dumped her purse contents onto the bed. A cockroach fell out and scurried under the pillow. She took no notice, too drugged to focus. His stomach rolled.

"I saw you at the café," she said. "Who's your target this time? The big black guy?"

He had to do something, and it had to be done now.

Chapter Ten

Alena hobbled into her boss' office with trepidation. It was bad enough that her leg throbbed like mad after standing for six solid hours, but to sit and listen to his whiny voice was a bit too much to bear. She had already missed lunch. If he went on one of his long dissertations, she'd miss her only chance to grab a bite to eat before a classroom of residents gathered for their weekly lesson.

"This better be important," she mumbled as she closed the door.

More than important. Dr. Julius Hoffman, head of radiology, never got off his butt if he could help it. He'd meander into the reading room when he wanted an opinion on a travel brochure. Like she gave a damn. Otherwise, he hobnobbed with the almighty in administration or went to meetings to sit and feel important while contributing his measly two words to justify wolfing down a half box of donuts. When the State Board of Health wandered in for inspection, he'd show them around before passing them off to her. Her natural charm won their approval every time, he claimed.

Bull shit.

In all fairness, he wasn't totally useless. She had complained about the cameras, and the man screamed bloody murder.

"You wanted to see me?" she asked.

Julius Hoffman looked up through thick spectacles. The man always sat higher than he stood, and today was no exception. She wouldn't be a bit surprised to see his feet dangled under the desk.

"Yes, come in, Alena, and sit down."

She flopped into a leather chair, grateful for the moment's rest.

"I suppose you're wondering why I called you here."

A little. What words of wisdom would she hear today? At least travel brochures didn't cover his desk. She waited.

"You know I'm thinking about retirement," he began. "The missus and I discuss it almost every night."

She muffled a groan. The same speech. Should he? Shouldn't he? When? Was he ready? Was there enough money?

Alena let him ramble. It felt wonderful to get off her feet.

"What you may not know is, I'm recommending you for this job."

Maybe she should invest in a new pair of shoes. That would help her sore feet.

"Alena, did you hear me?"

His words jolted her. She did indeed hear. "Me! I'm not qualified, Dr. Hoffman."

"You are more than qualified, Dr. Nichols. You've helped me with several budgets so far, the staff loves you, you have no problem scheduling procedures, and you interpret x-rays better than anyone I've met in my vast career. Why do you suppose I placed you in charge whenever I took a day off?" A smug expression covered his face. "I already sent the letter of recommendation to the top brass. With that said—" He paused to lean forward on his desk. "The doctor's ball is fast approaching. To my knowledge, you have never attended. I think it's high time you put in an appearance at the hospital's biggest social convention."

Panic struck. Her chest tightened, her throat closed up, and she was pretty damn sure she stopped breathing. *Oh, no!*

"I don't like going to those affairs, Dr. Hoffman."

"What you like and what is necessary are two different things. I want you to get my job because you deserve it. That means you need to show your face outside of the reading room, play a little politics, that sort of thing. You have a nice personality, and those stuffy board members need to see it. That won't happen until you socialize with them. Alena—" He paused, his wrinkled face serious but kind.

"I realize life hasn't been fair to you, but you are young with your whole future before you. I want to see you happy. If it's a man—or a woman—who will bring out that happiness, then please go for it. If it's the idea of a promotion, then go for that, too. If, however, you have no desire to be head of radiology, tell me now." He sat back and waited for her reply. She stared with amazement at the diminutive man with thick spectacles.

"I'm very flattered," she said. "Can I think about it?"

"No. I want you in this chair. If you flat-out refuse, then there's nothing more for me to say."

Wow. She never expected this. At her age even. Her mind raced through the possibilities of a management position. A challenge she never anticipated. She could do it. Of course, there was the potential of rejection. "Thank you, Dr. Hoffman. I will accept the position if offered to me."

"Good. Now, get out of here, and I'll see you at the ball."

The ball. *Oh, God*! Her throat closed up again.

She stood to her feet. "Thanks for removing the camera in the reading room."

He grunted. "It should never have been placed there, nor your office. I complained to the upper brass."

"Did you find who authorized the installation?"

"No. They're looking into it. It's amazing how documents suddenly vanish. Nobody knows anything any more." He peeked up at her. "I wouldn't want to work with a camera on my back either."

Whoever authorized the cameras had covered their tracks. She had a sneaky suspicion that Joe was behind it. The big question was why? Just to watch the love of his life?

She shuddered at the thought.

When she returned to her office, Alena made a frantic call to Nan Bauer. She begged her friend to meet for an early dinner in the hospital cafeteria. For the first time in her life, she couldn't concentrate on x-rays. Her class of residents had gotten a half-fast lecture that probably confused the hell out of them.

"What am I gonna do?" she cried. "I can't go to a ball! I'm so damn insecure these days, I could break down and cry."

Nan stuffed bread into her mouth. "Relax. It's not the end of the world. You're insecure because of your stroke and that jackass of a fiancé who left you. Otherwise, you're normal. Eat something before your stomach goes into acid overload."

They sat with their dinner trays at a table in the doctor's cafeteria. Alena's nerves kept her from eating what little she purchased. Nan's full-to-capacity tray hadn't a space available.

"I haven't done this kind of affair in years," Alena said. "I don't even know what it feels like to dress up anymore. What should I do?"

"You should go out and buy a gorgeous gown."

"Someone might ask me to dance. I can't dance anymore."

"There is no physical reason why you cannot dance." She shoved a potato wedge into her mouth. "You may be out of practice and won't do any fancy footwork without strengthening that leg, but it's time you revved up your happy feet." She shoved in another potato wedge. Her cheeks bulged like a chipmunk. "Stop making excuses. Eat your dinner."

Alena looked down at her tray. "I don't know why I got the steak. I hate steak."

Nan chewed until her chipmunk cheeks disappeared. "I got steak, too, which was stupid. Our cafeteria cooks it until you can reline the bottom of your shoes." She tried cutting it to prove her point. "Maybe it really is shoe leather, and they're calling it steak." She threw the knife down with disgust.

"I can't do it, Nan. I'm not ready." Alena buried her face in her hands.

"So, don't eat the meat."

"I'm not talking about the meat," she complained.

Nan finished her dinner plate and pushed it aside. "In your mind, you will never be ready." She wiped her mouth. "I'm glad Hoffman is forcing you into this. You need to get on with life, dear girl. Do you want your pear?" Nan took the fruit without waiting for an answer.

"I don't have a date. You have a date. I won't go alone."

"So, ask Sam."

Alena sat back, aghast. "I can't put Sam through that! He'll be bored silly."

Nan bit into the pear. "I'm sure he'd do you the favor. Besides, no one will ask you to dance with that big Neanderthal on your arm. I'll ask him."

"You will not!"

"Look, he's coming in next week to have his cast removed. If you haven't asked him by then, I will."

"No, I'll handle it. He's my friend. I should be the one to ask. And he is not a Neanderthal!"

"All right already. Don't be so touchy. Are you going to eat your cookies?" She reached.

Alena slapped her hand. "Don't you dare touch my cookies!" Alena inspected her food tray. Her eyebrows shot up. "You drank my chocolate milk!"

"Yeah, well…" Nan checked her watch. "I've got to get back. Calm down. I think Sam will surprise you."

Alena wasn't in the mood for any more surprises. If Sam couldn't go, so be it. She wouldn't go to the ball. Period.

She sat there and sulked after Nan left, playing with food she wasn't in the mood to eat. Nan was right. She needed to get on with life. Johnny was gone. Her stroke was behind her. She had managed to regain all of her motor functions. Physically, she could do anything. Mentally…well, her last night with Johnny was hard to dismiss. What if it happened again? What would she do?

She shook her empty milk carton and frowned.

The staccato of an overzealous newscaster caught her attention. She glanced up at the television on the wall to see a reporter screaming above utter chaos behind him.

"The scene is pretty gruesome," he shouted. "We advise you to look away."

Who were they kidding? They showed the scene in full color.

Dear Lord, what a mess! A woman had fallen five stories to her death, splattering her guts everywhere on the alley cobblestones. She had used a chair to break the window of her hotel room and jumped. The chair had landed on a homeless man sleeping in a cardboard box and cracked his skull. A cab driving down the alley swerved to avoid her body and slammed straight into a utility pole. One chain reaction after another. The reporter wanted to win a Pulitzer Prize so he broke through the police barricade for close-ups. *Uggh.*

"The victim has been identified as Christine McCullen from Los Angeles."

Alena froze. A coincidence, of course. A common enough name. Especially in Philadelphia where so many Irish had settled.

Los Angeles, idiot.

No, the reporter made a mistake. They wouldn't say her name without notifying next of kin first, right?

He repeated it again. No mistake. She had to be Sam's ex. Alena shot out of her chair and hurried from the cafeteria. She flew into her office to call him.

His phone rang. She paced. It rang some more. Voicemail kicked in. "Call me," she said.

A text message came back. *Later.*

She couldn't keep her eyes off the television after that. She read an x-ray then would run to the patient waiting area to catch the latest news.

A video came on showing a man with a cell phone to his ear pacing the hotel hallway. It was Sam. His body language revealed agitation before the screen went black. The reporters dissected the footage in their usual repetitive way, but it was a cheap-ass hotel. The owners never adjusted for power outage on the camera recorder. Date and time was last year at best.

"That's all we have," the newscaster said. "The police are looking for this man. If anyone can identify him, you are urged to contact the Philadelphia PD."

Aw, shit. Did they believe Sam killed his ex-wife? What should she do? Call the police?

No, she would wait for Sam to call. She already knew his ex wasn't an angel. She had summoned Sam to the hotel for a reason.

Sam called a few hours later and asked to meet in the lobby.

"It really was your ex?" she asked. They sat together on a lounge sofa away from other visitors.

"Yes. What a nightmare. She came out to seek revenge. I went to her room to talk. The more we talked, the wilder she became. She got so strung out, I stepped into the hall to call my boss. She had pills everywhere, Alena, plus crack and heroin. I told her if she didn't return to LA, I would call the cops and have her busted on drug charges. She refused so I stepped out. My boss suggested a hospital. Then I heard the crash in her room. That was when the chair went through the window. By the time I broke down the door, she had already jumped. The police were right behind me. My cell phone record recorded the proper time, so I was cleared."

"Why did the reporter say the police were looking for you if you were there?"

"*If it bleeds, it leads* scenario. The reporter knew I was with the police, but that wouldn't make headline news, would it? It wouldn't give him the exposure before the camera. Suspicion of murder is more newsworthy than suicide." He ran a hand through his cropped hair. "She jumped to frame me, of that I'm certain. She was hell-bent on destroying me when I was in LA."

The big guy looked so distraught...and pale. She rubbed the back of his neck. "Go home, Sam."

"Yes, I'll go home. Christine has no other family so I'll make some burial arrangements. I should let her rot in the morgue." He stood to his feet and took her with him. They hugged. It was the first genuine hug since the start of their friendship. She melted against him in a way that wasn't appropriate in a lobby full of people. She didn't care. She also didn't want him to let go.

Was she ready to change the rules regarding their relationship? Sam felt so good, but so did Johnny and look where it got her.

She reluctantly pulled away.

Chapter Eleven

The days passed. The news media let the suicide fade. Other blood and guts stories took its place. Christine had become another drug related statistic, only a number, nothing more.

Alena guided her car into its assigned parking slot to see little Mrs. Johnson, her next-door neighbor, fuming while sitting on a chair. The old woman often sat out on a nice evening with a book in her hands. Ninety plus and still active. She did everything herself except drive and that last detail only because her '87 Volvo died. Tonight, however, the book rested unopened on her lap while pursed lips wrinkled an already-wrinkled face.

"You don't look very happy," Alena said while stepping out of the car. "Anything wrong?"

The little lady grunted. "That hussy is after your man."

"My man?" Alena followed the direction of Mrs. Johnson's glare. Sam stood in front of his car talking to a woman dressed in clothes three sizes too small. They showed every curve God gave her. "Who is she?"

"Hmmpf! Our local tramp. The bleach blonde of the complex. Bleached one too many times, I can tell you. She moved in right after you. She's done every man in this section, even some of the married ones. Young, old, she doesn't care as long as they pay the money. She's after your man now."

"He's not my man, Mrs. Johnson. Sam and I are friends."

"Well, as a friend, you oughta go save him."

Alena laughed. "He might not want to be saved."

The old woman gasped. "You can't possibly believe he'd prefer her over *you*, do you? She changes men like she changes her underwear—if she wears any, and judging from what I see, she ain't wearing any. I'll bet my Social Security check that the woman carries every sexual disease known to man."

Alena watched the woman play her games with Sam. Provocative games. She leaned over his car hood to give him a full view of her impressive chest. She wiggled her ass to draw his eyes to the crack in her butt emphasized by cutoff shorts a trifle too cutoff. Sam stood talking, his huge arms folded across his chest. What he did with this woman was his own concern although a pang of anger rose from deep down. She also had this overwhelming urge to run over to scratch the hussy's eyes out.

The reaction puzzled her. Sam had a right to do whatever he pleased, even if it was with the complex tramp. "It might be his chance to get laid," she said. Even the words hurt.

"Oh, dear Lord, not with her! He's got you for that. She's trash, plain and simple." Mrs. Johnson slapped her book to make her point. "You know—" Her eyes turned into slits as she wagged an arthritic finger. "She was waiting for him. As soon as he came out of his apartment, she zeroed in. He's a strong-looking stud, I'll admit. He must be pretty good in bed."

Alena stifled a laugh. This wasn't the first time her

ninety-plus neighbor showed an interest in sex. She had often expressed regret at the lack of functioning sex partners in her age group. She considered a seventy-year-old a boy toy.

"Where's this woman live, Mrs. Johnson?"

"At the end of your man's building. She needs to be on the end. She's got men coming and going at all hours. I can't imagine what it's like to live next to someone like her, all the constant in and out. She needs a revolving door." She touched Alena's arm. "Are you sure you don't want to help him out?"

"He's a big boy. He doesn't need my help."

The old woman shook her head in disagreement. "That woman is a pro. She'll hook a man before he realizes what happened. A lot of men can't think once their hormones start to dance. Besides, you owe him one."

Alena stared down at the little lady. "Owe him for what?"

"He stopped a prowler by your door. It was that night he showed up wearing a tuxedo."

The bruise on his knuckle! Why didn't he say so?

"He probably didn't say anything so as not to worry you," Mrs. Johnson continued. "My kind of man."

"Was the prowler drunk, Mrs. Johnson?"

"Oh, I don't know. Your man threw him in the back of a car, and the car drove him away. It didn't look like a cop car."

Alena stood speechless. Sam had said the guy went into an end apartment. Why would he lie? Who was the prowler? The weasel man? If it wasn't a cop car, who was it then?

All these friggin' questions were giving her a headache.

"Uh-oh. The bitch is gonna make her move. Your interruption will give him a chance to pull back."

Sam was a man capable of taking care of himself. He didn't need Alena's help. However, Mrs. Johnson had made a good point. Either Sam wanted the hussy's attention or he did not. It wouldn't hurt to try.

Alena activated her phone and dialed. She watched him look down at his belt then return his attention to the woman. He even rotated to face away from Alena.

"I don't believe it!" Mrs. Johnson said with a gasp.

"So much for a rescue." She put her phone away. "Obviously, he wants what the woman has to offer. I'll see you later, Mrs. Johnson."

The woman offered Sam sex. Alena was far from offering Sam anything but friendship. She had a hard time pushing that simple fact out of her mind.

She entered her apartment and experienced a surge of anger. She threw her cane across the living room. Her purse followed. *What the frig is wrong with me?* She and Sam had agreed to be friends. Nothing had changed…except the hug in the lobby that had felt so right. That hug made her realize how much she missed the strong arms of a man.

Oh, hell. She wasn't ready for anything more than a hug. So what if Sam talked to a bleached blonde who made a living hooking? It was his business.

Remember your rules. Don't get involved. Don't fall in love. Why couldn't she listen to herself? Did she want her last night with Johnny repeated? All the pain? The anger?

It could happen.

And it could snow in July, too.

****

Sunday came. A food shopping day. Alena sat rereading her list when a knock sounded at the door. She hesitated answering when she spotted Sam through the peephole. She had sensed betrayal after seeing him with the hussy. For the life of her, she couldn't shake it. She'd agreed to be friends. Friends did not engage in sexual activity. She couldn't fault the man if he wanted sex.

Ignore the door. He'll go away. Yeah, right. He'd see her car.

He knocked again, a more persistent knock. Oh, what the hell. She opened the door.

"Hi," he said with a shy tilt to his head. "I thought you might like a walk in the park."

"Actually, I'm on my way to the supermarket."

"Great. I'll come with you. I can use a few things."

She stood there studying him. "I don't recall inviting you."

"We need to talk, Alena. It's important."

"I've got other shopping to do."

He stepped in, forcing her to step back. The aggressive maneuver surprised her. "Please."

Determination covered his face. He wasn't going to let her win this one. "Oh, all right. You drive."

"Glad to. I owe you some beer. I'll buy that while we're out. Ready?"

"No. Why did you hide the fact that a prowler was near my door?"

His brow cocked. "Who told you?"

"Mrs. Johnson. She saw you throw him in the back of a car."

"I didn't want to worry you. You've got enough going on."

Too much unfortunately. "Was it the weasel man?"

"No, someone else. An off-duty cop was driving by. He took him in."

That explained the car anyway. She let the anger subside. Her other questions would wait until later. She grabbed her list, cane, and purse in that order. They walked together across the parking lot to his car. As he pulled out, he said, "Where are we going?"

"The new shopping center. I wanted to check out the restaurant on the end."

"Sounds good. We'll do that before we shop. I'm starving."

Why was all this happening to her? She lived a quiet life alone. No one had ever bothered her before. Suddenly, she had men following, popping up from behind her vehicle, sneaking around her door. Ever since Sam walked into her life. Was it a coincidence?

Somehow, she didn't think so. Alena felt a powerful sense of trust in him. Maybe she had let her guard down too soon.

They settled into a booth in a far corner of a busy Mexican restaurant. After the waiter took their orders, Sam leaned forward, his voice low.

"You, no doubt, saw me talking to Odessa."

She had a feeling this was the topic on his mind. "Odessa? The name fits."

His lips twisted with irony. "Charming, isn't it? She has a porn site, too. I already checked it out. Whew, hot stuff."

No wonder the woman was so popular in the complex. Men had the opportunity to check out the merchandise before use. "What you do with this woman is your business, Sam."

"I'm apologizing for ignoring your phone call. I saw you talking to the old lady."

"I called to see if you needed rescuing." It had hurt when he ignored the call. It shouldn't have bothered her, but too many damn feelings were surfacing these days.

The waiter returned with drinks, chips, and salsa. They munched a few before Sam spoke again.

"Odessa is out of my league, Alena. I would have welcomed the rescue if the woman hadn't aroused my interest. It seems the news coverage about my ex prompted her to make an offer."

Alena held up a hand to stop him. "If she propositioned you, I don't want to hear it. If you spent time with her, I don't want to hear about that either. It's best if we keep certain things private between us." She cocked her head. "It's in the handbook."

A little smile curled his lips. "She propositioned me all right but not in the way you think. You have something she wants."

Alena sat back, stunned. "I don't even know the woman!"

"But you both knew Johnny."

Chapter Twelve

"*Johnny!*" Alena realized she said it too loud. She sat forward, voice low. "John Goodhart? My Johnny?"

Sam studied her, studied her long and hard with a grim, watchful expression. "Odessa offered me a generous reward for a memory card Johnny gave you."

"A memory card?" She blinked with surprise. "He didn't give me a memory card." She gasped. "Was that what the weasel man wanted?"

"Yes, he and the man outside your door were both Odessa's men. I questioned her about them." Sam ate a few more chips before continuing. His voice changed to one of nonchalance. "How well did you know Johnny?"

She thought she knew him quite well. A busy Ear, Nose, & Throat specialist in an established practice. Money in the bank. A charmer for sure. She hesitated with her answer. "I was going to marry him." She choked on the words. As if that explained the problems of the world.

"Tell me about him," he insisted. "Was he acting strange before your stroke?"

She toyed with a chip. "Moody would be a good word. He was worried about something. He never said what. It started before his trip to Vegas. When he got back, it was even worse. He sulked and argued and never came to a point. We were at constant odds. Maybe he wanted to break off our engagement and didn't have the guts to tell me." She watched him. "I'm about to find out I hardly knew him at all, I assume."

Sam nodded. "Odessa and Johnny were—" He paused, his gaze glued to her face, "involved. The memory card contains photos of their time together, photos that she preferred stay hidden."

Alena's mouth fell open. "I don't believe that!"

"I'm repeating what she said, Alena. It's her word against Johnny's since he isn't here to defend himself."

She almost married a man who slept with a whore? No, she couldn't believe it. "What makes Odessa think Johnny gave it to me?"

Sam ate a few more chips. His movements were slow and deliberate. Too slow unfortunately. Her nerve ends twitched.

"Johnny told her he hid the card," he continued. "He never told her where. She assumes he gave it to you."

"Johnny would be out of his mind to give me a card with porn shots. I'd have him strung up and quartered. She should ask Johnny to hand it over. I'm sure he took it with him." She said it with disgust. *Talk about a life turned upside down.* Johnny and Odessa. All captured on photos. *Uggh.*

"Odessa can't find Johnny either," Sam said. "He packed up and left her, too."

What was it with that friggin man? A love-em-and-leave-em sort of guy? His disappearance at such a critical time had dropped her straight into a depression. She snapped at anyone who tried to help. Her mom. Her dad. Nan. It took a long time before she snapped out of it.

"I don't have a memory card, Sam. I don't even

have a computer in my apartment." She stopped, eyes wide. "Is she the woman who trashed my furniture?"

"She admitted it, yes. She had a lot of time to search through your stuff."

"Then she must realize I don't have it."

"She's convinced you do. And no, you will not report her to the police. She's willing to make amends for the furniture if you give her the card."

The waiter returned with their food. She looked at her plate of tacos and realized she had no appetite. Sam dug into his burritos without hesitation.

"Did Johnny leave you anything, Alena? Anything at all?" He said it with a mouthful of food. "What about his office at the hospital? Did he leave anything there?"

"He was in private practice. The only thing he had at the hospital was a locker in the OR changing room. I'm sure he cleaned it out."

"But you aren't certain."

"I've no interest one way or the other."

"Is there a way for you to check?" He shoved more of the burrito into his mouth.

"You shouldn't talk with your mouth full. You might choke, and I don't feel like working."

He swallowed. "Noted. Are you going to answer my question?"

She reflected while picking at her refried beans. "If he didn't clean out his locker, the staff would have done it for him. The locker contents would be stored in Lost and Found, but it's been two years. I'm not sure how long they'd keep it." She sipped her drink. "You should check his office to see if he left anything behind."

"I already did. The receptionist remembers his mother picking up a box after he disappeared."

"His mother!" She fell back. "His mother died years ago!" She started. "Unless he lied about that, too."

He sipped his beer. "We won't know for sure until we find the card."

"Why?"

He looked at her after shoveling in a mouthful of Spanish rice. "Why, what?"

"Why are you helping her? You're a bank president. You can't tell me you need the money."

"To keep you safe mainly. I don't know what this woman is capable of doing. I don't trust her."

"She could have asked me first."

He made a face. "That would be awkward. The woman was sleeping with your fiancé. She asked me to search your place even if you denied having it."

"You can search my place if you want, but it would be better if she went looking for Johnny and asked him personally. I know I don't have it. Everything in my apartment is new since she trashed my old stuff." Well, except for the sweeper anyway. High time she got herself a new one.

She tasted the taco. Not bad. She took a bigger bite. "I'll check with Lost and Found tomorrow. If I find anything, I'll call you."

"I'd rather be with you."

She took another bite of her taco while studying him. "Don't trust me either?"

His smile was brief but strained. "I trust you, sweetheart. It's just that I have a bad feeling about all this."

He wasn't the only one who had a bad feeling. What if Odessa had told the truth? What if she and

Johnny were intimate and took pictures of it? He was engaged, dammit! When was he going to reveal his secret relationship? After the wedding?

No, she still couldn't believe it. She wasn't so friggin' dense then, and she sure as hell wasn't now.

She should have ordered a stronger drink.

"All right, *sweetheart*," she said with emphasis, "I'll call you from the hospital tomorrow to set up a time. We'll go to Lost and Found together."

She had more than a bad feeling. Something was wrong, and she didn't understand why.

****

They met as arranged and encountered the same scenario. John Goodhart's mother picked up his personal possessions over a year ago. A scrawled G. Goodhart signed the release.

"Johnny's mother is listed under the social security death index," Sam said. "It has to be Odessa."

"I don't understand why Johnny didn't pick up his own stuff or have it forwarded." Alena scratched her head. "Nothing makes sense."

They entered the lobby.

Alena started. The salt and pepper haired man sat in a lounge chair by the door. He nodded to her as he turned a page on his newspaper.

"Who's that?" Sam asked.

"He saved me from the weasel man in the garage."

Sam nodded his approval. "I'll have to shake his hand. After Odessa, I'd be suspicious of anyone who approached you."

Alena guided Sam to the side windows away from the patrons in the lobby. "What now?" she asked.

Sam took her hand and gave it a squeeze. "I'll talk

to Odessa. She may have to hire a private investigator to find Johnny. In the meantime, keep looking. If Johnny gave you anything—a key to a box, a confusing letter—anything, Alena, it might give us a clue. You could have it and not know it. The card could be hidden anywhere."

Alena shot him a glare. "The answer is with Johnny. You, Odessa, and I know it. Find Johnny and you'll get your answers. For the record, I don't give a damn about this memory card. It's Odessa's problem, not mine. If you're siding with her, then the two of you can take a hike." She yanked her hand out of his and turned to leave.

"Alena, wait." He grabbed her arm.

Surprised at the sudden grip, she stared down at it. He dropped his hand and cleared his throat. "I want you to know that I believe you," he said. "If Odessa approaches, I want you to call me. If anyone else approaches, tell me about it. Don't hesitate under any circumstances. Is that clear?"

She was a doctor. Her training included the detection of vocal variations. She heard some definite variations in his tone. What was he hiding?

"What's going on, Sam?"

"I don't want you hurt, and I don't want Odessa near you. Is that clear?"

She nodded. She didn't understand why he said it, but it enhanced the deep-seated feeling that something was terribly wrong.

Chapter Thirteen

Her moment of truth. Did she have the guts to go through with this? Was she woman enough to accept defeat if handed to her?

Alena paced back and forth across the grass debating those questions. Her cane thumped with her, gathering dirt and loose grass along the way. She resembled a lab rat stuck in a cage with four walls of nothing for entertainment. Only she paced in the wide-open space of the park with a view of the lake and its ducks and geese. A peaceful scene. Serene and calm. Unlike her nerves. A sense of entrapment enveloped her. She didn't want to do this. She wanted to forget the whole damn thing and refuse the promotion. Why did she agree to go?

Too much had happened too fast in the past several weeks. Sam for one. Odessa. A memory card. The questions were mounting, her nerves were near the breaking point. And worse. She should not have feelings for Sam. Hell, she wasn't sure she trusted him now, but every time he looked at her, her insides flipped, and *that* more than anything made her mad.

Calm down. There must be a reasonable explanation.

For what? Her growing feelings toward Sam or the mystery surrounding her life? She would welcome any answers at this point.

Alena stopped pacing to focus on the lake.

Another beautiful evening for everyone to come out of their apartment. Couples strolled hand in hand. Lots of couples today. She was a couple once. She missed it.

Really now?

No, she didn't want to be a couple again. Out of the question. Promises of love ever after and all that. Johnny had promised his love and look where it got her. She and Sam had the perfect arrangement, and she intended to keep it that way.

Focus, girl, focus. Look at the sky.

Yes, a beautiful sky. Not a cloud in sight. The temperature perfect. Memorial Day came and went. It put the summer season in full swing.

She loved summer. It was the main reason she asked Sam to meet her by the lake. She could watch the ducks on the water, smell the freshly cut grass, hear the birds singing in the trees. She could have waited in the parking lot, but she missed the lazy days of her youth. No cares. Lots of freedom.

It was hell to grow up.

What if Sam refused to go to the ball? What if he had a prior commitment? Who else would she ask?

No one. It was Sam or nothing. She wouldn't go. She just wouldn't go.

Her damn mind struggled with too many doubts. Was her relationship with Sam changing? She knew the answer before she asked the question. He had become part of her life, someone to talk to and confide in.

You confided in Johnny.

The realization shot a dagger straight into her heart. Was Johnny really involved with that woman? What about the photos on the memory card? Was it true?

It didn't sound like him. They had planned a wedding together. They almost bought a house. Did he have a perverted hobby that involved sex and porn? If so, why would he jeopardize the career he struggled to build? Even more puzzling, why didn't he ask for the engagement ring back? The gem alone had cost twelve thousand dollars. The ring sat in a safe deposit box because she hadn't a clue what to do with it.

So many questions, so few answers. Johnny had the answers. She turned away from the lake.

She started. Joe McMann from the hospital was walking on the asphalt path. He had his head down and looked to be talking to himself. His gait was jerky, a nervous kind of walk that looked half-undecided where he should put his next step. He wasn't in uniform. He wore baggy clothes that made him look thinner than he was, like a teenager waiting for his body to fill in the gaps. She even expected to see a skateboard tucked under his arm.

"Hi, Joe."

Her voice jolted him into the real world. Recognition passed onto his face, and he forced a nervous smile.

"Hi, Dr. Nichols. What are you doing here?"

She surprised him, and he looked downright guilty about it. Did he already know she lived in the area? If so, he was taking his crush on her a little too seriously. "I'm waiting for someone. What are you doing here?"

"Also waiting. My girlfriend lives in that apartment complex over there. She doesn't like when I come early." He glanced at his watch. "Ten minutes to go."

He twitched as he spoke. He couldn't stand still

either, shifting from foot to foot as if the ground was too hot under his untied sneakers. It was an odd coincidence that his girlfriend lived in her complex. Everything was an odd coincidence these days.

Joe's cell phone rang. He fumbled in his haste to answer, bouncing the phone in his hands like a juggler. He answered. "Great! I'll be right there!" He beamed. "She's ready for me. I'll see you later, Dr. Nichols." He ran toward the complex.

Good. She wasn't in the mood to have Joe around when Sam approached. She was edgy enough thinking about what to say and how to say it without making a complete ass of herself. She checked her watch out of nervousness. Sam said he would meet her as soon as he arrived home. He never gave a time. She never asked for one either.

Again, she started. A man sat on a bench on the opposite side of the lake. He held a newspaper up to hide his face, but there was no mistaking the attractive head of salt and pepper hair. Was it the same man from the hospital? Her gut said yes. This was more than a coincidence. He was following her. The question was why?

Oh, my God. Another Odessa man. No wonder he insisted on taking the weasel to security alone. All he did was set him loose.

"Alena!"

She turned to watch Sam walk toward her. She liked the way he carried himself. He moved with confidence and just a bit of a swagger. A big boy swagger. A don't-challenge-me-or-I'll-break-you-in-two swagger. She particularly liked the sound of his gravelly voice. It had a calming effect on her frazzled nerves, something she needed right about now.

He came alongside. "What's up?"

"We're friends, right?"

What a stupid way to begin. She practiced every opening line in the book, and this was her least favorite. Naturally, she blurted it first.

"Of course, we're friends. You should never doubt that."

On a personal level, she doubted many things these days. Her stroke had shot her self-esteem out a window. Her fiancé had packed up and left without a concern for her recovery. She had yet to start dating nor had any semblance of a relationship with a man. Both scared her to death, just as much as this damn ball!

"I need a favor," she began. She stopped to stare. "Your cast is off!"

"Yeah, yesterday." He elevated his hand to open and close his fist. "I guess I'll have to wear a tie again." He placed his hands side by side for comparison. "My fist shrunk."

Alena took his hand in both of hers and palpated. "Sore?"

"Tender. I have to do exercises to strengthen it."

She held onto his hand and turned it this way and that. It was a strong hand and callused, a hand that offered strength and protection. When she realized she caressed more than inspected, she looked up and met his gaze. The hazel glowed with amusement. She released his hand and cleared her throat.

"What's the favor?" he asked.

"I need a date for the doctor's ball. It's formal and will be very boring so if you refuse, I won't get upset." *I'll just jump off a bridge and die.*

"I'd love to go."

"You'll be surrounded by drunken doctors and—"

"I'd love to go."

She stopped. "You would?"

"If I'm going to have this incredible woman on my arm, yes." He paused with one blond brow cocked. "You're not going to be a drunken doctor, are you?"

"I hope not." She relaxed. "You really want to go?"

"With one stipulation. You must dance with me."

Her mouth dropped. "Nan told you!"

"That you were a fabulous dancer before your stroke? Yeah, she told me. I'm sure some of it is still in you."

She made a face. "I don't want to embarrass myself. It's bad enough my boss requested I play politics with the upper brass." She watched a couple of joggers run by on the asphalt path. She used to run. She used to do a lot of things. "He wants me to get his job. I may endure this formal affair for nothing. They could still deny me the promotion."

"If I were you, I'd go with the intention of having a good time. Nan said you haven't been on a date since your stroke."

Alena frowned. "Nan talks too much."

"She's your best friend, and she loves you. She threatened physical damage to my hand if I so much as harmed a hair on your head."

Alena chuckled. "She could do it, too. All right, I'll dance with you provided it's a slow song."

"For a chance to hold you in my arms, woman, you have a deal. Besides, I'm not the greatest dancer. I always feel like a monkey jumping around. Slow songs are good for me."

Two little boys tackled each other by the lake. Alena expected them to roll straight into the water, laughing and giggling all the way.

"What do you say we take a stroll?" Sam suggested. "It's a nice night."

"How about a short stroll. I've been on my feet all day."

He looked down at her with concern. "I've a better idea. Let's skip the walk and head back to the complex. You look tired."

She readily agreed. They started back.

She snapped her fingers and turned toward the lake, toward a certain bench. It was empty. The man from the hospital was gone.

"Something wrong?" Sam asked. He came alongside.

"I'm not sure. Do you remember the man in the hospital lobby who helped me with the mugger? He was here, on that bench over there. He's following me."

Sam looked around. "How do you know it was the same guy?"

"He's got a great head of hair. Hardly something I would miss." She frowned while scanning the area. "Considering how many people are interested in me these days, I assume he's another Odessa man. I can't figure out why he would follow me though."

"I guess in case you take the memory card out of your purse and wave it in the air. He could pounce." He stared across the lake. "He's gone now."

"You scared him away."

"Grrrr! Me strong like bull. Will tear him into tiny pieces." He puffed his chest out.

Alena laughed. She grabbed Sam's good hand and

urged him toward the complex. "When I see him at the hospital, I'll ask why he was here."

"Maybe he lives in the area."

"Maybe." She doubted it.

"Was I your last choice?" Sam asked.

"For what?"

"You know, your last choice for the ball?"

For the first time, she caught a hint of insecurity on his face. It showed in his eyes, and it surprised her. "I asked no one else, Sam. I trust you to help me through this. No other man will do."

He said nothing and kissed her hand. His lips sent a flow of warmth that she refused to shake off. It felt nice.

When they reached the complex, he spoke. "I told Odessa that you don't have the memory card. She didn't believe me."

She tugged on his hand to stop him. "If Odessa already has a porn site, why is she so worried about the photos with Johnny?"

He studied her. "You're too damn smart."

"I'm asking a valid question, and you know it."

They continued toward the complex. "I already thought about that question. I don't intend to ask her for specifics. For one, I don't believe she'll be truthful. Like I said, it's her word against Johnny's." He stopped her before they reached her door. "Have you ever heard of this town called Cape May? It's in New Jersey. I hear it's an interesting Victorian town."

Her brows shot up. "You like Victorian?"

"Well, after you showed me that house, I got a little curious about the style and did some research. Cape May links popped up everywhere I went. It isn't a style you see often in California, especially in LA. So, how about it? Have you heard of this town?"

"I can drive there blindfolded, Sam. I love the place. It's about a two and a half hour drive from here. Back roads. That's the way I go anyway."

"No Atlantic City Expressway?"

She shook her head. "Too far out of the way and too isolated. I hate that road. I never take it."

"Then how about a day trip to this Cape May? You can show me around."

She pondered the offer. It was a hard one to refuse. She hadn't been there since before her stroke. Should she? The man would be half-naked and an eyeful to behold. Her libido wasn't dead, just dormant. Oh, hell. She needed to stir up her insides anyway. "It will be a long day trip, but yeah, I'll take you. When?"

"When's the doctor's ball?"

"In two weeks."

"Then how about this Saturday? Are you game?"

She was more than game. He offered her a chance to return to her favorite place. "I'll call you to set up a time." With a wave, she entered her apartment.

Something felt wrong. The pillows on the sofa weren't where she placed them. The letters on her desk were shifted to the side, the chair itself halfway out. Her little Victorian houses were not centered either. Someone was here. She sensed it. Even more, she smelled him. It wasn't Sam's aftershave touching her nose. The big question, was the intruder still in the apartment? She called Sam.

He ran back. "Something wrong?"

She explained her suspicions. His brows shot up with surprise.

"Stay right here by the door," he commanded. He disappeared into the bedroom. After an eternity, he returned.

"No one's here now" He inspected the door lock. "No forced entry. Windows all closed and locked. Maintenance maybe?"

"Why would he move my pillows?"

"I can't answer that. Do you want to call the cops?"

"And tell them what? Nothing's missing that I can tell. Stereo and TV are still here."

"Then maybe you're imagining things."

"I smell his aftershave. Musk." She threw her purse on a chair. "It must be Odessa again. I'll bet she had one of her cronies come in looking for the memory card. You said she didn't believe you."

"A logical assumption." He frowned. "Damn stupid maneuver if you ask me. Maybe we *should* call the cops, put her on record, that sort of thing."

"No. I don't have the memory card, and she needs to know it. I'm surprised this happened. She already searched my stuff in storage. She must realize all this is new." She let out a long breath. "I feel a little better about it anyway. Thanks for coming back, Sam."

"I can stay for a while if you want or you can come back to my place. You don't have to stay alone."

His concern was touching if, however, unnecessary. "No, I'll be all right. I'm not afraid."

"Okay then. Don't hesitate to call me."

She wouldn't think of it. She already had his number on speed dial.

Chapter Fourteen

Sam walked into the bar feeling out of place. He never did the bar scene these days. A food place with a bar, no problem. A bar for the sake of a bar, no. Little men picked on big men when they got drunk. They always had to prove themselves, and Sam was a good way to do it. They never won, of course. Sam was too big and too well trained for most men, let alone a little one. It took a broken eye socket and a few busted ribs for them to learn the lesson. He looked around.

He could use a good fight right about now. He was so friggin' mad. Nothing was going as planned with this job. Too many variables coming into play. If he kept Alena alive through this mess, it would be a bloody miracle.

A drunk plowed into him. Tempting but Sam guided him over to the side and plopped him into a chair.

It was a typical bar scene. Bad lighting. Smell of booze. Women hanging on men. Men fondling women. A jukebox played. No one danced. Noise levels were tolerable. He spotted the guy he came to meet and sat alongside him at the bar. He ordered a beer.

"Would you care to explain yourself?" Sam asked.

The man sipped his drink. "Timing was off."

The salt and pepper hair stuck out in several spots. His shirt had window tracks caused by a body too large to squeeze through the opening. Small wonder the aluminum frame survived without being bent from his weight.

"Sorry, Sam. Donovan asked me to do it. He's getting worried."

"Well, if you two had clued me in, I could have sat on a bench with her. She thinks it's Odessa's cronies."

The man nodded. "Thanks for helping me out the window."

Sam sipped his beer. "You'd be in handcuffs if she didn't call me back. I'm grateful she's got a good head on her shoulders." He glanced at the crowd at the other end of the bar. Two women were eyeing them like raw meat. *Yeah, here we are, two studs at the bar, mingling with the rest of the losers.* He suddenly hated his single life. "I suppose you found nothing."

"Not enough time."

No startling revelation. A simple text message could have kept her by the lake. "You'll have the whole day on Saturday. She's taking me to Cape May." He paused to draw in a deep breath since his blood pressure came spiraling out his ears. "Doesn't Donovan trust me?"

"As you said, Sam, she's got a good head on her shoulders. Donovan thinks she's fooling all of us."

Sam looked at him. "What do you believe?"

Dave ate a few pretzels before answering. "I've watched her for several weeks now. She's an eat-work-sleep kind of gal. I'm siding with you. I don't think she has it. We're watching her cell activity. Nothing. The hospital computers have a monitoring system in place where nothing the staff does is private. If she's involved with all the traffic, she's doing it another way." He sipped his drink. "Donovan's worried you might be getting in over your head."

Sam was way over his head with this job but kept his mouth shut. Alena Nichols was beautiful, intelligent, and available, but the job came first. Her attributes were secondary. That's what he repeated to himself anyway.

"McMann showed up," Dave said. "He talked to Alena for a few minutes before running toward the complex. I don't need to tell you whose apartment he ran into."

Sam guzzled his beer and ordered another round. "No one is more dangerous than a young man with not enough blood flowing to his head. He doesn't realize the woman's like quicksand. She'll suck him in and then laugh while he disappears."

Dave agreed. He waited for the bartender to place their beers and move on to the next patron. "Odessa searched your place."

"Yes, I know. She saw the surveillance photos, nothing else. I guess she doesn't trust me either."

"She wants the card. We want the card, and Alena has no idea what she's involved in."

Sam had come home from work and made the intruder discovery. He'd found the bleached strand of hair she left behind. "Alena doesn't deserve to be in the middle of this mess. I'd like to tell her."

"Yeah, well, you know you can't do that. We get paid to find things, not to get involved." Dave sipped his beer. "Sorry to hear about your ex. What made her jump?"

"Something I said." He watched a man put his hand down a woman's pants. She giggled, the stupid shit. "There wasn't any love between us anymore. She turned into the devil incarnate after our divorce. I took this job to get away."

"What was it, high on coke?"

"Coke, meth, sleeping pills, all swallowed down with whiskey. The autopsy report was unbelievable." He popped a few beer nuts into his mouth. "I can breathe a sigh of relief once I land in LA now that she's dead. You ever been married?"

"Twice. I'm currently available."

Sam looked at him. "Twice?"

"It's the job, man. Women expect a guy to be home every night. Isn't that why you divorced?"

Dave hit the nail on the head. Christine had become demanding; the drugs made her combative. Sam's marriage had reached a point where he didn't want to go home at all. "Any kids?"

"Two. My first wife made sure I got her pregnant. Learned my lesson with the second one."

"How often do you see your kids?"

Dave guzzled his beer. "Not enough. My schedule and theirs don't coincide."

Sam grunted. "You sound like my old man. He was never home."

"Not many of us are, Sam. A word of advice. If you marry again, don't have kids. Keep yourself available for some of the better jobs."

"I liked being married," Sam said. "Before Christine got into drugs, it was nice to go home to someone who cared. The loneliness gets to me after a while."

"I know that feeling, but marriage has a way of dragging a man down. I don't think I'll try it again. I can always hook up with a woman. That one over there for example. She's been eyeing me since I walked in."

Sam glanced where Dave indicated. "The redhead? She looks a little used and abused."

"Better that way. No muss, no fuss. One night stands are the way to go."

Sam couldn't stand the one-nighters. It involved sex with a total stranger. The high relieved the loneliness for an hour...tops. "Alena knows you're watching her," Sam said. "Maybe you should shave that head of yours."

"Women like this hair, man." He ran a hand through it as if to prove a point. "I'd rather be replaced than shave my head." He lifted his glass, saw it was empty, and sighed. He stood to his feet. "Saturday, huh?"

"Yes, Saturday. All day. Tell Donovan you'll have the time to search her place with a magnifying glass. But do it discreetly. She knew you were in that apartment the second she opened the door."

"How?"

"Women notice little things. A pillow not where she placed it. A piece of paper cocked. Be careful, will you? We don't want her spooked so she'll pack up and move away. Oh, and you might want to omit the aftershave. She's got a good nose." He sipped his beer.

The man slapped Sam on the back. "Thanks for the advice. Have fun in Cape May."

Sam caught his arm. "Don't you let her out of your sight. I don't trust Odessa. If those two thugs worked with Odessa and now McMann, who knows how many more are watching her."

"No worry. Even Donovan says that. I'd like to

know why Odessa is working with such amateurs."

"They're expendable. Plain and simple. If she worked with men as dangerous as her, Alena would be strapped to a chair and tortured." The vision angered him. He never killed for the hell of it, but Odessa could change that unwritten rule.

"I'll lay low," Dave said, "since she likes my hair." With a wink, he left the bar.

Sam sat for a few minutes nursing his beer. A mirror stretched along the wall in front of him. Years of cigarette smoke had clouded any semblance of a reflection. No one had bothered to clean it after the smoking ban went into effect. He struggled to see himself let alone the people behind him. Why did bars put mirrors up anyway? An old habit perhaps from the wild west days when every gunslinger had to watch his back. And speaking of watching his back...

A familiar head of straw strolled through the door. Odessa. She looked like a woman who belonged with this crowd. A tall, lanky young man followed her. He was in his early twenties, the stage where he wasn't quite a man yet. No bulk. His clothes hung on him and that more than anything made him resemble a teenager. They approached. Sam turned to face them.

"Following me?" he asked.

"My, what a coincidence!" Odessa declared. "Meet Joe."

Odessa's boy toy. Sam watched Joe enter her apartment several times already, always after another man hurried out half-dressed. Joe was a classic case of a young man with raging hormones doing it with a whore twice his age. The boy was so friggin' dense.

"Aren't you going to buy me a drink?" Odessa

slithered onto the barstool next to him.

"I think your date should do that. Is he old enough to drink?"

Joe's back stiffened. His dark eyes glared like daggers, eyeing Sam with venom. He motioned for the bartender who demanded a valid ID.

Joe's complexion turned a beet red as he dug through his wallet. When their beers arrived, Joe remained standing between them, trying to look big and imposing. He failed.

"What brings you here, Odessa?"

"This is my kind of place, Sammie. I thought I'd bring Joe so he can get a feel for the environment."

"Feel what? All the sleaze balls and hookers hang here. I'm surprised people aren't doing it on the tables."

"You're here, Sammie. Maybe that's what you enjoy." Her red lips curled into a sneer. "Bank presidents can have their little quirks."

She emphasized the last statement with a lift to her voice. She said it for a reason, and he wondered what she had up her sleeve.

"I had a drink with a friend."

No sense hiding it. She wasn't an unobservant woman, and coincidences were not a part of his job.

"He's helping me keep an eye on Alena." He admitted it because Joe watched the hospital monitors all day. He didn't want Dave replaced despite his head of hair.

"Nice to hear," she said. "How much does he charge?"

"Too much." He threw a twenty on the bar and stood to his feet as a little man plowed his way through the crowd toward him looking determined and cocky.

Here we go again, he thought with irritation. Maybe this was a chance for Joe to show his worth to Odessa because Sam McCullen sure as hell wouldn't.

Without another word, he slipped out the side exit.

Chapter Fifteen

Their day together arrived. Alena drove. Sam sat back and enjoyed the sights. Of Alena mostly. She looked happy and relaxed. He wanted to believe because he sat in her passenger seat acting all manly in his swim trunks, but common sense kicked him in the ass. Their Cape May destination lightened her mood. Her brown eyes glowed, her smile spread without effort, and her hair blew in every direction from the open car windows. She was beautiful.

Even though she pointed out sights along the way, his gaze always drifted back to her. He enjoyed the sight of her more than any structure. Nan was right. Alena loved Cape May, and Nan deserved a big kiss for suggesting the trip.

His cell phone chirped. A text message. He read it. *Bidding active. BB promises delivery. Watch your back.*

Now, how the hell could bidding be active? Was Odessa playing with fire? Did she already have the card or did she encourage the bidding with the assumption that Sam McCullen would find it?

"Everything okay?" Alena asked with a slight cock of her head.

The frown deepened. "I wish I could tell people I don't want bad news while I'm out enjoying myself."

"Should I turn around?"

"Hell, no!" He wouldn't cancel this trip even if the

big boss ordered him back into town. This woman was his for the day, and he intended to enjoy the moment.

She studied her rearview mirror. "It's hard to tell if we're being followed. Cape May is a one-way-in, one-way-out town."

He had discussed that detail last night with his men. They hung further back as a precaution. He would prefer not to have a tail, but she was too important.

"I may as well break it to you after your bad news text," she said. "Someone broke into my office Thursday night. They ransacked everything."

His head snapped. "Did the hall cameras pick them up?"

"Funny you should mention that. All the cameras on our floor malfunctioned that night."

"Convenient," he growled. "Any other offices get hit?"

"Just mine. It must be Odessa again."

Or Joe McMann. Who else could disable the cameras and play the innocent?

"Anything missing?"

"Nada. However, I have patient files in my office. If someone took one of those, I won't know until I need it. Administration was not pleased."

"That woman is starting to get on my nerves," he said with irritation.

"She's determined."

More than determined. With bidding active, desperation should follow. That's when people made mistakes.

"I didn't spoil your mood, did I?" she asked.

The smoothness of her voice was like a sedative. The anger toward Odessa dissipated. His lips broke into a half grin.

"I wouldn't give a shit if our apartment complex burned down right now. You and I are going to enjoy this outing and forget about Odessa. Clear?"

She smiled back at him. "Clear."

The town of Cape May proved to be everything he expected. Street after street of Victorian houses, old intermingled with new, some private residences, others bed and breakfast. Alena pointed out a newer Victorian compared to one that withstood the test of time. Her bubbling enthusiasm changed her from the quiet calm doctor to a happy carefree woman who enjoyed her tour guide duties. He also suspected that he caught a glimpse of the woman before the stroke. He liked what he saw.

"What?" she asked. "Am I talking too much?"

Oops! He sat lost in dreams, dreams of her in bed on cool sheets, dreams of waking beside her in the morning. Every day, he struggled with the necessity of keeping her at arm's length coupled with the strong desire to wrap her tight against his chest. Every night, he would lay awake wanting her, and every night, he told himself it was wrong.

He shook his head in answer to her question, but his smile remained. He had better say something before she bopped him one.

"You're an excellent historian, Alena Nichols. Do you realize you're giving me dates for some of the construction down here?"

She cringed. "Sorry. I get carried away."

She had carried him right along with her, and he loved every second of it.

"I want you to know that for the first time in years, I'm having fun," she said. "I want to thank you."

Yeah, Nan Bauer deserved a really big kiss.

A short time later, Alena stopped to obtain beach passes. He sat in the car to wait and let his gaze wander over the crowds.

Summertime at the Jersey shore. Droves of people on the beach, along the streets near the shops, and on the boardwalk, which was really a concrete walkway. A family atmosphere without question. Parents carried beach chairs and blankets while children ran ahead swinging plastic buckets and toys. A few scantily clad women strolled by. They paused to ogle him with appreciative stares. He flexed the arm muscle dangling out the window to make them drool.

Alena returned to the car as this exhibition ended. She looked from him to the women. "You don't have to hang around me all day."

His eyes turned into slits. "If you think for one second that I would leave you alone with all these hunky men around, think again, woman. As far as I'm concerned, you and I are on a date."

A puzzled expression crossed her face. Doubt followed it along with a subtle biting of her lower lip. He knew what flashed through her mind, but he didn't care. They were on a date, plain and simple. It was high time she realized it. However, to ease her doubts before she bolted, he straightened in the seat. "I'm your bodyguard today, Dr. Alena Nichols. I will fight to the death any dragon that comes near you, male or otherwise."

That worked. She gave him a warm smile and started the car.

"We have the beach tags, a picnic basket, and a blanket," she said. "If you're ready for the beach, I'll find a place to park down the other end. It's less crowded. You will notice that everything is metered." She opened the ashtray. Nothing but loose change. "I brought quarters."

Before long, he stood on soft sand looking out at the Atlantic Ocean. He stood mesmerized, blanket and basket in his hands, staring in awe. "Your water isn't *blue*! When did we leave the planet Earth?"

"If you want blue, you have to go to Bermuda." She grabbed his arm and led him down the beach. "I understand the Pacific looks nice."

"Compared to this, the Pacific looks like sapphires. Is it safe to swim in?"

"If it wasn't, we'd see a lot of dead bodies floating. How's this spot?"

Perfect. He wanted a little privacy with the woman for as long as he could get it. Judging from the popularity of the beach, privacy was at a premium.

Sam handed her the basket and spread out the blanket. He waited for this moment all morning. "All right, woman, I want to watch you take your clothes off."

"Dear Lord, Sam, don't say that too loud. There are kids everywhere." Then she leaned toward him and in a low voice said, "I want to see you half naked, too."

Just what he wanted to hear. He tore off his shirt with a bit of a flair. He already wore his swim trunks. He gave her a body-builder pose by puffing up his chest and arm muscles. "How's this?"

"Hot, Sam, very hot." She fanned herself. "I'll be fighting the women off you."

Alena threw her cane onto the blanket and undressed. She wore a functional swimsuit, red in color, one meant for swimming as opposed to sunbathing on the beach. It showed soft curves of proportional size but no cleavage. It did offer him an eyeful of leg.

"How's this?" she said and took a pose.

"You are a feast for a man's eyes, Alena." His voice cracked, dammit. "You would kill me if that were a bikini."

She fussed with her clothes to avoid looking his way. "You do have a way with words, Mr. McCullen."

She couldn't fool him. The compliment pleased her. It showed all over her face.

The furious shrill of the lifeguard's whistle caught their attention. Sam and Alena followed the direction of the guard's glare.

Alena shielded her eyes. "Two teenagers. They're out too far."

The lifeguard's whistle broke everyone's eardrums in his desperation to get the teenagers inward. His face matched his red swim trunks from the effort.

"Kids don't like to listen to authority," Sam said.

No sooner were the words out of his mouth when both heads disappeared under the waves. The lifeguard gave a signal with his whistle to the guards down the beach then flew off his stand and ran toward the water. Everyone jumped to a standing position to get a better view.

A woman in a red swimsuit flew past Sam and ran down the beach after the lifeguard. Seconds later, an SUV pulled up towing a boat. More red-suited lifeguards jumped out and pushed the boat into the water. All movements were coordinated and precise. He turned to comment to Alena when he stopped. He stood alone near the blanket. It took several more seconds to realize that the woman who chased after the first lifeguard was Alena!

"Hey!" He ran toward the water.

Two more lifeguards showed up. One stopped Sam. "We'll handle this, sir." He put a radio up to his mouth. "It's Alena, guys! Repeat, Alena's in the water! She's overtaking Ricky as I speak!" Then to Sam with a proud face, "Damn, look at her go!"

Sam stared in awe at the woman who swam strong and steady, surpassing the first lifeguard with ease. The drama created a dead silence on the beach as everyone watched and waited. When four heads bobbed above the waves, everyone gasped. When the boat crew hoisted the teenagers out of the water, the crowd cheered. Alena and the lifeguard hugged each other and like two synchronized swimmers swam toward shore.

As they approached, the remaining lifeguards ran into the water hooting and hollering. They lifted Alena onto several strong shoulders and carried her to shore. Cheers and applause from the crowd greeted them. The lifeguards hugged and kissed her then hugged and kissed again as one man passed her to the next.

One lone woman surrounded by muscled tanned bodies. Sam didn't like that part one damn bit. He felt somewhat better when several female lifeguards joined the crowd, but even so, he fought the urge to charge over there. Bad enough she had run past without him having a clue. What the hell kind of professional was he to let that happen?

He allowed enough time for this reunion of sorts before his nerves got the better of him. He approached. Their gazes locked. He recognized the plea and broke through the crowd. "Excuse me, ladies and gentlemen, but this woman is with me." In one quick sweep, he lifted her in his arms. She shrieked. The lifeguards cheered. Sam carried her toward the ocean.

"What are you doing?" she asked with alarm.

"You already took a dip. Now, it's my turn."

He dunked himself and her under the waves. The lifeguards cheered when they surfaced. The crowd applauded. Their show for the day. With her still in his arms, he carried her back to the blanket. He held her, reluctant to let go.

"You can put me down," she said.

He looked at her. So close. "No."

"Everyone's watching."

"Don't care."

She laughed. "Sam!"

"Oh, all right." He put her down.

Alena used a towel to dry off. Sam let the sun do the job. They stretched out on the blanket, she on her back, exhausted, he propped up on one elbow alongside. Water slicked her hair back. It darkened the color and made her eyes look lighter. Her lashes were just dark enough to accentuate the desert sand.

"Would you care to explain yourself?" he asked. "I suppose it's no coincidence that you're wearing the same style swimsuit as the female lifeguards. Now that I look a little closer, I see where a patch used to be."

"I'm sorry. I should have told you I spent my summers here as an instructor. I trained most of these guards." She put a flat palm on her chest. "Whew! I haven't done a swim like that in a long time."

"And do you realize that you *ran* out to the water while your cane rested all alone on the blanket?"

"Yes, and now I'm paying the price. I didn't think I

could do it." She smiled up at him. "Thank you for the rescue."

"You're welcome. I suspected you were about to collapse."

She closed her eyes. "I should strengthen this leg."

"Yes, you should unless you're preying on a guy's sympathy."

Her eyes stayed shut, but she smiled. "I never thought of that."

"It didn't work with me."

She looked at him and laughed. "I'll have to try another tactic on you, I guess."

He brushed sand off his leg. "Walking around naked should do it."

"Ha! In your dreams, pal." Her eyes sparkled. She closed them.

The damn woman was too beautiful, too tempting, and way too close. He bent down to kiss her. As before, her lips responded and damn if it didn't feel good. He wanted more than anything to get her in bed, but he dared not. It was essential to keep the relationship status quo, but with each passing day, it took more self-control, control that was essential for the job. That's why they sent him. He was the best of the bunch. Yet, he couldn't shake how damn miserable it made him. He might break all the rules with this one.

Alena smiled up at him. "I like the way you kiss, Sam, but you know I'm not ready for anything more."

"I'll take your lips any way you give them, Alena. Maybe one day, I'll break you down."

"Maybe. Don't count on it." She gave a quick peck on his lips. "By the way, that was a bit of a caveman routine you did."

He disagreed. "A caveman would toss you over his shoulder. I carried you to feel your bulges."

"And?"

"Very nice."

She laughed, an honest-to-goodness belly laugh that brightened her entire face.

"We could find a room and spend the night," he suggested while inspecting his nails. *So much for status quo.*

She gave him a slight pout. "Your chances of finding a room on a Saturday night in prime vacation time is nil, Sam." She closed her eyes. "A lot of these places will tell you that they require a three night stay."

"Rats." He would settle for one room, one bed, and one night with this woman. He sighed. "Just as well. It would be a night of sheer torture." And the only one-night stand he would absolutely enjoy.

She looked at him with a smile warm and inviting. "You say the nicest things, Sam McCullen."

"I'd like to do some nice things to you, too," he growled.

The uncertainty returned to her face. He even detected fear. Why fear? Of him?

"How come you don't live down here?" he asked to change the subject.

"Because the area has one hospital. I had a lot to learn. I chose the big city hospitals for the experience."

"Makes sense. How about now? Any desire to relocate?"

She shook her head. "Real estate is out of my reach down here. I'm better off where I'm at."

He calculated five mil and better for anything along the beach. Maybe two mil and better a few blocks inland. Conservative estimates for sure but far lower than west coast properties. Out of his reach, too.

He watched a little boy dig a hole in the sand. He worked with a feverish pace until half his body disappeared. On his way to China no doubt. Satisfied, the boy threw in a yellow truck and covered it up. In twenty minutes, his parents would wonder what happened to the toy.

"I'm hungry," Sam said. "What's in the basket?"

She sat up. "Sunblock first."

He groaned.

"What's the matter?"

He glared at her with as serious a face as he could muster. "You must realize that I'm having a hell of a time fighting the arousal you cause in that swimsuit. Yes, I know, I see no cleavage, but your ass is nice and round, and your legs—" He whistled.

"That's why I didn't wear my bikini."

"Bikini? You have a bikini?" He broke into a sweat. "You shouldn't have said that, Alena." He rolled onto his stomach to hide the growing bulge in his swimsuit.

She nodded as she grabbed the sunblock. "I understand, Sam. I'm a doctor. I know these things."

Oh, God! She was so cute! He wanted to wrap his arms around her and never let go. He wanted to kiss her until she gave in. Most of all, he wanted to feel himself inside her.

Sheer torture indeed. He held his breath while she smeared the sunblock onto his back. She did it with a gentle massage that stimulated him even more.

And she expected him to do the same to her? God help him! He would have some erotic dreams tonight!

Chapter Sixteen

Alena rushed around as if she chased her head across the rug. God forbid she should break out into a sweat. There wasn't time for another shower. This was the evening for the doctor's ball. Sam would be at the door any second. She couldn't find her necklace, couldn't find her shoes. She had set everything out for easy access, but of course, her mind drew a blank. She had picked both the necklace and shoes up and put them down somewhere. She hadn't a clue where. Nerves blinded her. She shouldn't have asked him, shouldn't be going, and shouldn't have bought this eye-popping gorgeous gown.

She had a more demure gown in her sights, one that showed less cleavage and far less shoulders. Naturally, she fell in love with this one. The color was lavender silk, strapless, and formfitting to the point of having her body poured in. It was way too sexy for a night out with a friend.

Their day in Cape May had brought an irreversible change to their relationship. After baking in the sun for a few hours, they strolled through the shops, munching on caramel popcorn and ice cream, playing games in the arcade and having a blast of a time. He'd found a ceramic Victorian house for her collection, a pretty little piece that lit up from its own internal battery. She would treasure it above all the others because Sam bought it for her.

They had animated discussions as they walked. They passed an antique shop; they discussed antiques. They passed a record store; they discussed music. When one person too many broke between them, Sam grabbed onto her hand and never let go. He growled at anyone who tried to break his hold. It felt nice. The sense of trust returned. She had this big man watching over her, and she didn't give a damn about anything else. By the time they returned to the car, a closeness had developed that she knew would never go away.

Tonight would increase that closeness because a current passed through them now, a current she recognized as stimulating and frightening. It led to relationships, and relationships meant commitment. It meant love, sex, and ecstasy.

She wasn't ready for any of it.

When he had suggested they spend the night, she almost told him several options. She worked with so many people in Cape May. They wouldn't hesitate to give them a room for the night. But she couldn't do it. Would she ever be ready?

She found the necklace. Thank God for small favors.

Why wasn't she ready? She had run into the water, her cane forgotten, her weakness pushed to the back of her mind. Her primary goal was to reach those kids before the riptide carried them out to sea. What was so friggin' wrong that she couldn't dismiss her last night with her fiancé?

It couldn't happen again. As a doctor, she understood the odds. As a woman, the fear of uncertainty overwhelmed her. And what about Sam? He had indicated his desire for more than friendship. But why should she?

Because she felt something from him, that's why. Every time he touched her. Every time he looked into her eyes. A protective feeling, full of trust, full of love. The sense of security he gave was intoxicating. Did she misread her own signals? Was it hormones dancing? Or was it a subconscious desire to fall in love again?

She found her shoes. They were on her feet.

Maybe she needed a psych consult, someone with the experience to look into her head to figure out what the hell was wrong.

The doorbell rang.

Too soon. Too soon. Another moment of truth. A night that could change her life forever—if she let it. She opened the door.

The gown had the affect she expected. Sam's mouth fell open. "You look fabulous!" he gasped.

This was why she bought the gown. For Sam. She shouldn't have, but she did it anyway. She wanted him to feel proud. She wanted him to feel as if he had the most beautiful woman in the world on his arm.

"Thank you," she said. "You look good, too, but I had the advantage of seeing you in a tux before. And that's a much better bowtie you're wearing. Come in. I need to ask you a favor."

Sam stepped in but quieted her voice by placing a finger against her lips. "I'm glad you're not engaged anymore. I wouldn't be standing here if you were. You take my breath away."

"Don't try to sweet talk me, Mr. McCullen, but thank you. I haven't dressed like this in a long time. I'm glad it's with you." She touched his cheek. Then, what the hell, she reached up to kiss his soft skin. She lingered to suck in the intoxicating aftershave. When she backed away, Sam stopped her by taking her hand.

"I have two very special requests, Alena Nichols. The first is to leave your cane home. You have my arm all night, and I expect you to use it. Besides, at the first sign of drunkenness, you might start swinging and crack it over my skull. The second request—" He leaned close and flashed her a devilish grin. "You tormented me in your bathing suit, and now, you will torment me in this gown." He lifted her chin. "Can a friend break a rule by taking a bite of your shoulders?"

Alena sucked in a breath so hard, her ears popped. "Sam, I am so sorry. I knew I shouldn't—"

He quieted her lips again. "You bought the gown because it changed you from Dr. Alena Nichols, sensible radiologist, into the sexiest woman I have ever seen."

"Oh, God!" The blush that shot to the surface of her skin flushed her face, ears, and all of her neck. Everything burned.

Sam's eyes sparkled while his lips spread into a warm smile. "Friends help each other. You'll hold onto my arm, and I will take a bite sometime during the night. Is it a deal?"

His tone was playful and teasing. She relaxed. "It's a deal. That's what friends are for."

"Right." He pointed to the Victorian house display. "Which one did I buy?"

She wasn't surprised he couldn't pick it out. Men remembered the absurd, like a fossilized dog turd. "Dead center, Sam."

He nodded his approval. "What did you want to

ask me?"

"Can we give Nan a ride?"

"Sure, but I thought she had a date."

Alena checked the contents of her purse while answering. "He canceled at the last minute. Last night in fact. He decided he'd rather climb a mountain in Colorado."

Nan was fit to be tied. She had called the man every name in the book including ones Alena never heard before. If he ever showed his face again at the hospital, Nan would boil him in oil.

"So I'm going to have two beautiful women on my arms," Sam said with a low whistle. He rubbed his hands gleefully. "I'm a lucky man."

"If you can handle it."

He cocked an eyebrow. "Good point." He pursed his lips as his face scrunched into a frown. "Let me make a quick phone call, Alena." He activated his cell phone and stepped outside.

****

Two beautiful women. Both highly educated and available.

Heaven help him.

Alena looked stunning in her lavender gown. She had her hair pinned up and held in place by a diamond-studded something-or-other. Sam had no idea what women called those things, but it looked nice. It held her light brown hair off her smooth shoulders while a perfectly sized necklace drew his gaze straight down to her soft breasts. Sexy as hell. Other men's eyes would do the same. That made him proud, proud that she would hold onto his arm, proud that she chose him to help her through this evening.

It felt wonderful.

Sam pulled his car onto the circular tarmac of the country club and scanned the outside perimeter. The man he expected stood off to the side dressed to the nines in a black tux. He appeared apprehensive and with good reason. Sam had mentioned nothing about his phone call to the two women despite Nan's threat to stay home and iron. Then she complained about being a third wheel until Alena convinced her that an ample buffet table waited. That got Nan into the car faster than a slingshot.

As the two women stepped out, an audible gasp escaped from Nan's throat. Nathan Donagher emerged from the shadows and approached.

"What are you doing here?" she cried, half choking on the words.

Nathan showed a set of bright white teeth. "I'm your date."

Nan whirled toward Sam, her eyes like fire. "You called him?"

"Yes, and don't put any blame on Alena. As you can see from her face, she's equally shocked. I am incapable of handling two incredible women at the same time so I sent for backup."

Nan's eyes grew wide. The fire died, and she laughed. She turned to Nathan. "All right, you big lug, I won't let you dress up for nothing. I'm yours for tonight, but you have to behave yourself. You are not to call me squirt, is that clear?"

"I'll be the perfect gentleman." He held out his arm, and together they entered the country club.

Alena turned to Sam who smiled after them. Her eyes sparkled.

"You're sneaky, Sam McCullen. I wondered why you drove so slow tonight. You were giving Nathan enough time to get dressed and over here."

"Yeah, timed it right, too. They make a nice couple, don't you think?"

"Nan's going to eat him alive."

"Nah. Nate can handle her. He's been trying to get her on a date since they met at the café. This is the perfect opportunity for them to get acquainted." The valet handed him a ticket for his car.

"Our time tonight is special," he continued. "I'm feeling selfish. I'd rather not share you with anyone, not even Nan." He held out his arm. "Shall we go in, Dr. Nichols?"

Alena smiled at him and took his arm.

Chapter Seventeen

At last. Sam had Alena in his arms. He had endured the required socializing, met every stuffed shirt from administration on down, and was politely ignored by every Tom, Dick, and Harry who had to see Alena Nichols up close. She was more than a radiology doctor tonight. She caught everyone's eye. She moved with a grace that belied the need for her cane. Her dress, her hair, her makeup were model perfect. She was polished and beautiful.

The woman generated an insatiable curiosity. He knew nothing about her lifeguard years. When he thought about it, he knew very little about her past. His report had covered the present and hardly very much of that either. What else would he discover besides a tender woman who didn't deserve to be mixed up in this mess?

They'd had a great day in Cape May. She had talked about her life living in a shore community, the friends she made, the carefree years before med school. He had talked about the California beaches, and how there was no comparison. As much as she coaxed, he wouldn't talk about himself. What could he tell her without revealing his purpose on the east coast? Besides, she wouldn't talk about Johnny. So, they were even. He had settled for an enjoyable day with a wonderful woman who made it harder to concentrate on his job.

Sam held her tight while they danced. It was a nice slow number where her head rested on his shoulder. Her scent was intoxicating, her hair, her shoulders, both playing with his libido. He wanted to hold onto her all night, but of course, that wouldn't be wise. The job came first. Always the damn job first.

He must be out of his mind.

"You turned down a lot of offers to dance," he said. "I didn't catch your excuse."

She lifted her head. Those desert sand eyes reminded him of home. Every time he looked into them, the homesickness seeped into his heart. He wondered if she would like California.

"I told everyone that my first dance must be with you," she said. "I'm counting on you to not let them cut in."

"That's a given, woman. I'll crush any man who tries to take you out of my arms."

She laughed, but he meant every word. He never felt more possessive in his life.

He eased her head onto his shoulder as they moved in a slow rhythm. Her body leaned in a way that surprised him. It also pleased him. Her softness, so wonderful to hold, stimulated a part of his anatomy that only a strong zipper could contain. Hard as it was to admit it, he wanted this moment to go on forever. He kissed her hair.

"You impressed a lot of people with your bank title," she said.

"Big deal. I'm one of four presidents."

"They don't know that." She lifted her head to look at him. "Now that you've had enough time at it, how do you like your new job?"

"It has its moments." He hated the job. It was a role to be played, nothing more. His responsibilities were minimal, a pretense to keep the staff from questioning.

One part of his job was not a role: his relationship to the beautiful doctor. What would she say when she discovered his true identity, his purpose for coming into her life? He sensed love from her now. She fought to keep it bottled, but it was there for him to see, to feel in her touch. Why did she fight it? Why was she so afraid to fall in love again?

"I want to thank you for being so patient," she said. "I know you're bored."

"I am not bored. It's been…an interesting evening."

Far better than the anniversary party he had attended but with undeniable similarities. Another bunch of overdressed people pretending to have a good time. Same stodgy music. Dear Lord, was it the same band?

He almost chuckled to himself. This time, he didn't care about the music. Slow songs meant closeness. Her enticing shoulders, tanned from their day on the beach, stood inches from his lips. He wanted to tell her how alluring she appeared, but he dared not.

One dance led to another until the hours passed. Fast, slow, it didn't matter. She stayed in his arms. Her head stayed on his shoulder. At one point, he swore she fell asleep. When her grip tightened on his bicep, that signaled the time to leave.

"Where's Nan?" She scanned the crowd.

"She and Nathan left an hour ago." Straight into a bed more likely. "Let's go."

Alena threw her heels off before he put the car in gear. She rested her head on the seat headrest and faced him. She looked so tired…and content.

"Do you have family, Sam?"

She tried earlier to get him to talk, and he held back. He wanted to know so much more about her, and it was only fair if he reciprocated. He maneuvered around a slow-moving vehicle before answering. "I have a sister, Jennifer. She's younger by two years. Married with two boys. My mom is still around, a very active seventy-year-old. Lives by herself not far from Jen. My dad died years ago."

"All in California?"

"Yes."

"Do you miss them?"

"I suppose I do. I played with my nephews when I wasn't working. Went to a few ball games, that sort of stuff. I always wanted a family to call my own, but that didn't happen with my ex-wife. My all-consuming career pretty much prevented it. What about you?"

She yawned. "Mom and Dad are alive and well and living in Erie, Pennsylvania—that's where I grew up. No siblings. Lots of cousins."

"Why do you live so far away?"

Her gaze drifted beyond him, out his side window as if he wasn't there. "I grew up as a pageant child," she began. "My mother dressed me like a doll and paraded me in front of judges. It was fun at first. I was four years old and strutting around like a grown-up. I endured a bunch of modeling and speech classes, singing, dancing. You name it. My mom had big dreams for me. The first movie star in the family or at least commercials." She ran a finger along the leather console separating them.

"It doesn't sound like happy times, Alena."

"It wasn't. By the time I was nine, I rebelled. Big-time rebelled. My mother and I fought with the coming of every pageant. I begged my father to interfere, but he was afraid to go against my mother. When she realized my temperament was not going to win any prizes, she accepted defeat and allowed me to grow up normal." She shifted in her seat to stare out the front window.

"For years, I struggled with the stigma of being a pageant girl because my mother wouldn't let anyone forget it. I hurt her, I know, but I was living her life, not mine. I wanted to be a doctor, not a movie star." She fell silent while they waited for a traffic light to change.

"College became my excuse to get away. I wanted to make sure I had my own life, away from my mother's friends and her pageant activities." Her gaze drifted toward him. "I gave it up. My mother did not. She helped other mothers get their daughters ready." She stared out the window again.

"Your experience wasn't a total waste," Sam said. "I never saw a woman more beautifully put together, full of grace with a fluid movement to her body. Your pageant training did that for you." He reached across the console to touch her hand. "You don't need that cane, Alena. It's time you accepted the fact." He wasn't sure she heard him. Her gaze stared straight ahead, unseeing. "What did your parents say when you told them you wanted to be a doctor?"

"They didn't care. By then, I was so far removed from their world." She turned to face him. "College was hard at first. The loneliness was awful, but I was determined to make it work. Then I met Nan. We became instant friends." She fell silent. She looked at nothing in particular until he touched her hand. She gave him a weak smile.

"After my stroke, I moved in with Nan. My mom came down to help. She wanted me to return home with her, but my life was here. Nan had to convince her to return to Erie." Alena straightened in her seat. "Johnny and I were kindred spirits, Sam. His father pressured him to become a lawyer and go into politics. Neither one of us had much of a childhood, and we connected because of that. I thought we were a perfect couple, everlasting love and all that." Sadness covered her face. She shook it away. "Do you think you'll return to California?"

He pursed his lips, hesitant as to why she asked. "I love California, Alena. It's where I belong."

"I see." It came out as a whisper.

What the frig is wrong with you, man? He gave her the best reason in the world to keep their friendship status quo. What woman in her right mind would give her heart to a man who could pack up and return to his home state clear across the continent, especially a woman whose fiancé scarred her soul by disappearing without a word?

"I won't lie to you. I will return to California when the time is right."

"I understand, Sam, really I do. Your wife is dead now. You left LA because of her. It's logical that you'll go back. You don't have to explain anything to me."

For some reason, he needed to explain it to himself more than her. He had come out here to do a job, not to get involved with a woman. When the job reached its conclusion, he could kiss the east coast goodbye.

"What happened between you and your fiancé?" He hated to push, but he had to know. "You didn't tell me everything."

She shot him a glare. "What makes you think there's more?"

"It's in your eyes. I see fear."

The glare died. Sadness drifted in. She turned away. "You're seeing things."

"I understand the abandonment issue. He left you at a critical time, and it hurt. I also understand your reluctance to fall in love again. I don't understand the fear. Does it have to do with Johnny?"

"Don't push, Sam."

Sam knew the details of John Goodhart's disappearance. Alena deserved to know as well. Only then could she face the fear that paralyzed her.

Odessa was right. Alena had the memory card. She just didn't know it. He needed to get his hands on the card before Odessa ordered her cronies to take drastic action. Alena Nichols was the one who could help him find it.

Sam pulled up to her apartment and escorted her to the door.

"I had a good time, Alena. Thank you for asking."

She opened her door before turning back. "You never took a bite of my shoulders."

He stepped back, surprised. "Do you want me to?"

"It was one of your stipulations."

"Stipulation or not, I can't do it." His voice cracked. "If my lips touch your skin, I'll lose it."

Her lips curled to show the devil within as she reached up to kiss his lips. He died and went to heaven. He wrapped his arms around her and pulled her close, sucking in all that she gave. When she leaned into him, he grabbed her hips and pressed them against his erection. A tremor shook her. She would pull away any second so his lips traveled her neck to the shoulders he had been dying to bite all night. A groan escaped from her lips, and she moved away. Her gaze was misty. He almost had her, dammit.

"You have to know how I feel about you, Alena. What would it take to get you in bed?"

"Patience, Sam, and to ask it of you wouldn't be fair."

She had the better self-control. This was without doubt the hardest case he had ever worked.

He kissed her lightly expecting nothing in return. He didn't get it either. "Good night, beautiful." He turned back to his car.

She got to him. He was a pro at his job, the best of the best, trained to resist the wiles of women. He had traveled the globe and slept with women connected with the case. He always said adios without looking back. Why did he drop his guard this time? What made Alena so special?

He knew why. He was in love with Alena Nichols and God help him when she found out the truth.

Chapter Eighteen

A whole week passed without seeing Sam. He said he had to go away on business. Alena didn't ask where. She didn't ask when he would return. She had reminded herself that they weren't a couple, and she had no right to know. He was a bank president. Management went to conferences, retreats, hoopla events.

Damn, she missed him.

It had left her in a vulnerable mood. Like a fool, she volunteered to cover a Saturday ER shift.

Alena sat munching on red licorice sticks in the ER doctor's lounge while flipping through a fashion magazine. The day was uneventful but busy so far. Her assignment included fast-track where the minor emergencies congregated. That meant head colds, cuts and scrapes, a stitch here and there. Stuff that generated a yawn.

The door flew open with a bang. Nan stormed in looking like a thundering black cloud. Her friend gave a curt hello and barreled into the locker room.

Alena glanced up at the clock. "Aren't you a little early? Your shift doesn't start for another hour."

Constant slamming was her answer. Nan Bauer morphed into a fire-breathing dragon when the black mood emerged. Something had set her off. Lord only knew what. The last slam, however, nearly broke an eardrum.

"What is wrong with you?" Alena complained. "Everything seems to set you off these days."

Nan slammed a locker in answer.

Alena already spent ten hours of her shift on her feet and was on a much-needed break. Up until this moment, she enjoyed the peaceful solitude the lounge offered, clearing her mind. Listening to Nan slam everything in sight did little to encourage rest.

"How's the weather outside?" Alena asked. Maybe a casual question would cultivate some calm. A loud grunt came in answer.

A whole week of this grumpy mood. Ever since the doctor's ball. She tossed the magazine aside.

"All right, I've had enough. What's wrong?"

"Nothing's wrong." Nan slammed her locker to confirm it.

The woman needed a happy pill. Nan never kept anything bottled up. She never hesitated to blurt out words without thinking, saying things she shouldn't, never giving a damn whether she put her foot in her mouth. No inhibitions whatsoever. Thankfully, the lockers were made of metal and not glass. "Get out here and talk to me."

"No."

"You can't keep this up. You're snapping at anyone who comes near you, me included. You're supposed to be a little more cheery for our patients and their families."

"Leave me alone."

The two women had never found the time to meet for lunch or dinner this past week. If Alena became available, Nan was not and vice versa. That meant grumpy Nan bottled her anger. Not healthy. Several staff members had already commented, and yesterday, Alena caught Nan snapping at a maintenance man. So unlike her.

At the risk of getting her head bit off, Alena tried a different tactic. "Are you mad at me?"

No slam in answer. After several minutes of quiet, Nan appeared in the lounge area. She looked tired and irritable. Her eyes showed the signs of insomnia with dark circles surrounding bloodshot eyeballs. "What's wrong, Nan?"

She kicked a side chair. She stared at it as if daring it to kick back. "Sexual frustration," she said at last.

Alena's brows shot up. "You! Really?"

"Yes, really."

She wasn't sure what to make of this piece of news. In fact, Alena wasn't sure sexual frustration belonged in Nan's vocabulary. "You have a list of men to call. Is something wrong with your phone?" She took another bite of her licorice.

"Nothing's wrong with my damn phone. Nothing's wrong with me. Everything is wrong with the universe."

An unexpected answer. And baffling. It left Alena with no retort. Sometimes, she wished she had studied psychology a little more in med school. "That doesn't explain your sexual frustration, dear. I can't help you. We may be best friends, but I have my limits."

Nan flopped onto a stool to put on her sneakers. She tied her laces. Not satisfied, she retied them tighter. That allowed little room for circulation to her toes. Alena made a mental bet that within three hours Nan's feet would fall off.

Finished with the shoelaces, Nan sat and stared at

the floor, looking dejected. An odd expression for her. Always so perky. Full of confidence. Alena let her sit. It presented a chance for the fire to die.

"I invited Nathan in after the ball," she said at last. "I thought a little sex would top off our evening. He didn't think so. He turned me down."

Alena sucked in half of her licorice and promptly went into a coughing fit. No man turned down spunky little Nan Bauer. She was every man's fantasy of sex without commitment.

Alena cleared her throat, wiped the tears from her eyes, and without hesitation, shoved the rest of the licorice into her mouth. "Did you kill him?"

Nan shuffled her feet. "Why would I kill him?"

"He had to be a first. Dear Lord, I'm shocked. Amazed. Flabbergasted."

"All right, don't go overboard."

"I'm sure he gave a reason. What was it?"

"He said I didn't know anything about him."

"You don't, but that never stopped a man before." She gasped. "Is he gay?"

"Gad, I hope not." She buried her face in her hands.

Nathan wasn't gay. He had looked at Nan with adoring eyes at the ball. To everyone's surprise, Nan had danced with only him all night. Others had tried to cut in, but she gave a polite smile and refused. Unusual for her.

Alena studied her empty licorice packet and wished she had bought two. "You should call one of your other studs. I'm sure they'll accommodate you on short notice."

"I don't want to." Nan glanced up. "I'm tired of

that routine."

It had to be age, or her hearing. Alena wasn't sure which. Nan was tired of calling a stud for a romp in bed?

Alena thumped the side of her head to clear her ear.

Nan continued to stare at the floor. She looked so down-in-the-dumps, like the world was coming to an end, and she could only sit and watch it happen.

"You've always been a free spirit, Nan. I don't understand the change. It's so unlike you." She stopped, eyes wide to popping. "Nathan got to you!"

Nan made a face. "Let's say the man has me stumped. He sounds educated. He conversed like an intelligent human being at the ball. He handled pointed questions with ease and created an air of mystery about our relationship, which, I might add, is non-existent. His clothes fit well, his SUV is brand new, and he lives in an apartment building that you and I can't possibly afford."

"So, what's the problem?"

She took an inordinate amount of time to answer. "I walked by his building the other day. I caught him rolling a big trash bin across the lobby."

Alena cocked a brow. "Is that supposed to mean something? I've pushed a mop once or twice in x-ray. I got housekeeping mad at me, but it was either that or let my patient break his neck. What did Nathan say?"

"Nothing. He never saw me."

"Well, maybe he was helping someone."

Nan jumped to her feet, the fire reignited. "He wore dirty coveralls, Alena. He's the damn janitor!" She paced. "He told me he was an unemployed computer programmer."

"He's got to eat somehow, sweetie. It explains how he lives in an expensive apartment building. That type of establishment may require a janitor to live on the premises. See? A logical explanation."

Nan grunted in answer. The pacing continued.

"Except it doesn't explain the short notice tux he wore," Alena pondered. "You could tell he owned it since it fit so handsomely."

The pacing stopped. A dreamy expression passed onto Nan's face as a slight smile touched her lips. "He did look handsome, didn't he?" She shook herself. "He could have borrowed it from someone in the building."

"Unlikely. What about the SUV?"

"He could have borrowed that, too."

She had an answer for everything. "All that put aside, it doesn't explain your unwillingness to call one of your studs to alleviate your sexual frustration. I guess you'll have to accept Nathan's disinterest in casual sex and forget him."

"Will you stop being so damn logical!"

"The man is not into you. Admit it."

"He wants a friggin' relationship!"

Alena started. "He said that?"

"Yes, dammit! It will never happen."

"Why not? He seems nice enough."

"I will not date a janitor!"

Well, well, well. This was an amusing surprise. It explained Nan's short temper and unwillingness to talk. Alena grinned. "The man got to you big time. Otherwise, you wouldn't be acting like this."

"Ha!"

"You should find out if his janitor job is temporary. It could be, you know. He may not be proud of what he's doing to put food in his mouth." Logic had its advantages after all.

Nan stopped pacing and stared down at the floor. "It's a plausible explanation." She pursed her lips. "You're right. He was embarrassed to tell me. Just like he was embarrassed to tell me he took out his own stitches."

Alena jerked. "What stitches?"

"He got hit with a pipe wrench and wound up in the ER a week before the ball. It saved him a lot of money by doing it himself. He'll probably get an infection and blame me." She dropped her chin onto her chest. "It's not like I'll see him again. I told him to get the hell off my porch, and I wasn't very nice about it either." She squared her shoulders and smiled. "You made me feel better anyway."

"Glad to help." Alena stood and tossed her licorice wrapper into the trash. She stretched. "I've got two hours left to my shift. I might think twice before I volunteer for another Saturday. I'm exhausted."

"You can't fool me. It's like old times. You love it."

Maybe. Just a little. She had a chance to talk to real people, moaning and groaning people.

The overhead intercom clicked. "Trauma: Code One! Trauma: Code One!"

The two women exchanged glances. Nan's face lit up. Trauma excitement. Multiple casualties. Constant chaos. Nan's forte.

Alena wanted to swallow the contents of an aspirin bottle. "I guess I won't be going home anytime soon."

Even so, her adrenaline kicked in. She grabbed her cane and followed Nan out the door.

****

She would never, ever cover a Saturday shift ever again! Her one shift turned into a double with no end in sight. They could bribe her. They could promise her the moon. Never again! She would bury herself in x-rays from here to eternity!

At least for the next three months.

Alena collapsed on the cot in the doctor's lounge with her body in total revolt. She had come in for the second time to change her bloodied scrubs and didn't have enough energy to put her shoes back on. Her left leg had turned numb hours ago. She damned near hit the floor in front of everyone. An orderly had caught her. She was ushered to the lounge to change and rest. Well, she had changed her scrubs but was too exhausted to rest. Hell, every muscle ached!

She'd set more bones tonight than she did in her entire career. They recruited any doctor who could sew on a button to stitch up some skin. The patients poured in. Two buses they said. It felt like two trains. The chaos was unbelievable.

Nan burst in full of energy. A whirlwind of untapped current. Nothing fazed her. She handled triage with the expertise of an old pro, directing the flow of patients through the doors with the skill of a traffic cop. Seven hours into her shift and still a ball of fire.

Alena peered at her. "Please don't tell me three more ambulances pulled in."

"No. We got word that minor injuries remain at the scene. You're going home."

"I can't move." She covered her eyes again with her forearm. "I don't even want to look at the clock."

"It's one thirty in the morning. That's why I got

you a ride. I'll put your clothes in a bag." She hurried into the locker room.

"I don't care if you got me a ride. I'm not moving. I'll spend the night here."

"No, you won't," said a gravelly voice.

Sam stood in the doorway staring down at her. He looked disheveled and sleepy. "When did you get home?" she asked.

"Three hours ago."

"Nan woke you?"

"Yes, I woke him," Nan said as she rushed back in. She carried a bag stuffed with clothes in her hand. "He's the one I trust the most to take you home at this hour. Get your shoes on."

"Put her shoes in the bag, Nan. She won't need them."

Sam reached down and lifted Alena into his arms. Words of protest failed her. She felt his arms before. She liked them then. She sure as hell liked them now. She melted against his chest. "You feel so good," she whispered. She nestled her head near his neck.

He kissed her hair. "You feel even better."

She knew what that meant, and she hid the smile it generated.

She fell asleep in his arms.

Chapter Nineteen

Alena popped open one eye to see daylight seeping through the drawn curtains. A quick glance at the alarm clock showed ten forty-five. She never slept this late. Then again, she rarely had a night like last night. A horrible shift. One patient after another had rolled through the doors screaming, crying, covered with dirt, glass, and debris. Blood everywhere. Their clothes had smelled of diesel oil. Those closest to the bus engine smelled the worst since the oil had nowhere to go but out. From here on, every diesel powered vehicle on the surface of the earth would trigger a memory of this one night.

She rolled over.

She was on her bed still dressed in her scrubs, tucked in and comfy. She sat up and stretched. Several muscles rebelled, and she recoiled faster than a new spring. *Ouch*! Her body felt like a train bounced her down the tracks all the way through two stations and back. She couldn't remember ever working so hard.

Never again. Absolutely, never again.

Then Sam had showed up. He held her with arms strong and protective. A different feeling from when he carried her on the beach. That maneuver was playful, a pretend-to-drop-you tactic. This time, security had flooded her senses. And more. She felt...love.

Oh, God.

She shouldn't have let it happen. She should have steeled herself better, avoided him more, worked more. But it was love, the one emotion she tried to keep buried. Every time they were together, her heart slipped into V-tach.

Entirely his fault. He had infiltrated her life until the inevitable happened. But friends could love each other, right? She loved Nan. She could love Sam in the same way. Love didn't mean falling in bed together. Love meant caring for someone, being aware of his feelings, all that stuff. What should she do? Ignore it? Pretend it never happened?

Later. She'd think about it later.

Alena swung her legs out of bed, thankful that the numbness in her left leg subsided. Her cane rested against the doorjamb out of reach, but she never used the cane in her apartment. A little voice told her to ditch it forever, to get on with life as a normal human being with ordinary hang-ups. But the cane had turned into an old friend. A safe old friend. A companion.

A crutch.

She wasn't ready to part with an old friend.

Alena scratched her scalp to fluff her hair and strolled into the living room. She should thank Sam for taking her home last night. Maybe her exhaustion brought out the feeling of love. Yes, a plausible explanation. A weak moment, a desire to feel the protection of strong arms, to have a man care for her. Every woman's dream.

She stopped.

Sam was still here! His large frame was stretched on the sofa, covering every breadth and width of it. His shoes were off and stood on the floor by his head. Her sweater covered his chest and looked more like a handkerchief than something to keep him warm. She tiptoed over and stood alongside.

From the moment they met, he had stirred so many dormant feelings. She had convinced herself that she could never trust a man after Johnny. She also believed she could never feel affection toward one either. She'd felt both for Sam McCullen. She fell asleep in his arms without a second of hesitation because her trust in him was real. He was so different from Johnny. Strong and dependable. Sensitive. Caring. Those were the words for Sam. He had generated feelings of longing, a persistence that grew as time went on. She sensed it now as she watched him sleep. He was a special man who had entered her life and made it feel right again.

Sam caught her wrist. Without opening his eyes or moving the position of his head, he coaxed her down onto the sofa, onto him until his other arm wrapped around her. He rolled her onto his side, trapping her between the back of the sofa and his body. His lips pressed onto hers, kissing with a warmth that she sucked in like a sponge. He nibbled on her mouth, his teeth bit her tongue. The tenderness overwhelmed her senses. She gave in and kissed back, melting against him in a way she hadn't done to a man in years.

His arms tightened in response, and he squeezed her to his chest so that no air passed between them. Emotions poured from his mouth to hers, powerful emotions she fought from the day they met. She let him have it in equal force, her body screaming with the sensations of pleasure, an awakening so long denied. Hands traveled. His. Hers. Her fingers traced along the muscles on his chest. His hand slipped into her scrub bottoms and squeezed while pressing her hips against his straining erection. She wanted him, dammit. *He wanted her*!

The last realization gripped her. Panic shot straight to her throat, choking her airway. She pushed on his chest. She pushed hard with all her strength until he gasped and hit the floor with a thud.

She vaulted across the room, forcing distance between them. He jumped to his feet, eyes wide, shock covering his sleepy face.

"Alena—" He stepped toward her.

"Don't come near me, Sam!"

He froze. "You know I would never do anything to hurt you."

"I can't let this relationship go beyond a friendship!"

"Why? You are looking at a man who loves you. I can't hide it anymore. I want to shout the words to the world. I love you. I have always loved you. I want to do what two lovers do. I want to taste every square inch of your body. I want to feel myself inside you. I want to love you, Alena. Tell me why you're afraid."

Defiance set in. She lifted her chin. "I am not afraid!"

"Like hell you're not. I see the fear in your eyes. Something else happened between you and your fiancé. What was it?"

"No—" Her voice cracked. She swallowed hard. "Maybe you should leave."

A red flush covered his face. "Wild horses won't drag my ass out your door. Talk to me!"

His anger was intermixed with uncertainty. He deserved an answer. She deserved to kick him out.

"You weren't supposed to do this," she said instead.

"Fall in love, you mean? How could I help it? You're so damn beautiful. I want to see you happy again, Alena. I want to erase the pain you so cleverly hide. Tell me why you resist."

Tears welled in her eyes. She stepped back. "I can't love you, Sam."

"Why? Tell me, dammit! You've kept it locked up too long. Free yourself, Alena. Spit it out!"

His words hit like a dagger. It twisted and gouged, forcing her to step further away. Only Nan knew her secret. A man would never understand, not even Sam. Yet, he was right. She had to let it go. Life would not begin again until she did. She struggled to form words.

"It's a painful memory, Sam."

"Try, sweetheart, please. For me."

Oh, God, this is hard. She clenched her fists to maintain a sense of control. "My stroke hit during intercourse. I became flaccid, a lump under Johnny, totally aware, but unable to move or speak. Johnny never noticed. He kept going, pushing for his own satisfaction. I was powerless to stop him." She choked on a sob as she met Sam's pleading gaze. "I felt like I was being raped, Sam, having sex against my will. It was a horrible feeling, one I have trouble shaking to this day. I couldn't stop Johnny. I couldn't even try!"

Sam stepped toward her, but she held up a hand and backed away.

"Johnny never looked at me," she continued. "He rolled over and fell asleep without once giving me a second glance. I wanted to kick him or at least spit in his face. I could do nothing but lay there. I finally gurgled loud enough to wake him."

The anger of that night surfaced in full force. She couldn't scream then, but dammit, she sure wanted to now. She bit her lip instead. "Johnny was devastated. I watched him pace like an animal waiting for the ambulance. He couldn't do anything to help me. Then, of course, the doctors reprimanded him for not getting me to the hospital sooner. I guess that was why he disappeared. He couldn't handle the guilt. I felt alone and abandoned, tossed aside like a used rag." She swallowed hard.

"I don't know what felt worse: the feeling of being raped, his leaving me, or the stroke that changed my whole life. It took me weeks before I got up enough guts to conquer my depression and fight the paralysis that wrecked my body. A paralysis, mind you, made worse because of a man who never even looked at me!" She said the last sentence with uncontrollable fury. Sam didn't deserve such anger. She closed her eyes for a few seconds before continuing.

"I hated Johnny for a long time. I hated him for leaving me, for not checking to see if I was breathing. He was so friggin' self-centered that night. He didn't care if I reached climax." She sniffed as she tried to control the boiling in her gut. "When I thought about him over the months, he was always like that, another self-centered man who never cared about his partner in bed." She wiped the tears from her face.

Sam stood in silence watching her. He looked lost and unsure, and she wasn't about to help him. She wanted him out of her apartment. She wanted him to stay. The conflict ripped her heart into shreds.

"Not all men are self-centered bastards," he said. "A man isn't worth his weight in salt if he doesn't satisfy the woman first."

Defiance set in again. She threw her head back. "So you say."

"Are you afraid intercourse would lead to another stroke?"

She nodded. "That and the fact that the man will let me turn into a cold slab of meat."

He shook his head in disagreement. "Life is full of chances, Alena. What are the odds of another stroke? An aneurysm you told me. What are the odds of another blown aneurysm?"

"I don't know."

"You're a medical doctor. You *should* know. You need to conquer the fear that built up inside you, sweetheart. The fear of commitment, fear of sex, fear of a relationship, and most of all, fear of love. You are a vibrant intelligent woman. You have a large capacity to love. It's what makes life worth living." He approached. She stepped back. He held up his hands in a gesture of surrender and stopped.

"You spoiled everything, Sam. You promised to be a friend, nothing more."

"I also promised not to get involved with another woman. My divorce wasn't a piece of cake. I swore to live the rest of my life as a single man. You changed all that."

He gave her a long penetrating look, both analytical and impatient. Did he expect her to dismiss that horrible night with a snap of her fingers?

"I fell in love in that dark x-ray room," he continued, "but you insisted on friendship. I went along with it because I thought, 'Fine I can handle it.' As time went on, I couldn't handle it at all. I think of you night and day. You cause me to have erotic dreams when I sleep. You creep into my thoughts no matter how hard I try to push you out. I love you, Alena. I want to make love to you now and forever. I want us to have children who have your sand-colored eyes and cute nose. And if anything ever happens to you, I will be there always. I want our life together to be happy, and I want it to be long."

She started, sniffed, and blinked. "Did you propose?"

"Hell, yes! I can't go on any more being just a friend. I want to be your lover, your husband. I want to be there when you fall asleep at night and when you wake up in the morning. I want to hold you when you're sad, protect you, do everything a lover and husband is supposed to do. But I want all of you, Alena. I want you to live for me and stop burying yourself in the past. In the beginning, I asked for nothing in return. Now, I want it. I want all you can give and more because I will give you everything I've got."

She sniffed. "I can't."

"You can't or you won't?"

She sniffed again. "You're asking me to put a lot of faith in you, Sam, and I can't. I'm not ready."

His jaw changed to granite. "No one will kiss your lips like I will. No one will love you as deeply, but I will not compete with Johnny's memory. When you're ready to let him go, you know where to find me."

He grabbed his shoes and left without another word.

Chapter Twenty

Sam sat on a bench on the far side of the lake in full view of the apartment complex. He read a newspaper as he waited, trying to appear as nonchalant as possible. If Alena should appear, he could bolt off the bench and head toward town. He could also meet her halfway.

Yeah, right. Like she'll come to you, buster.

The lookouts had reported his overnight stay to Donovan. The obvious was assumed. Sam had expected to be replaced, but Donovan said no. Replacing him now would leave Alena wide open for Odessa and her cronies. A dangerous situation.

Donovan had given Sam the get-it-together speech. The job came first. They weren't in the business to treat the lovelorn, and Sam's reputation was at stake. A kick in the pants for sure. He had let himself slip on this job, and he needed to correct it.

Odessa strolled toward him. She swaggered more than walked, using her round hips to an advantage. She caught the eye of every man around, generating thoughts of rough sex at a high price. She caught the eye of all the women, too, but those eyes glared with scorn. For a change, modest clothing covered her ample curves, modest by hooker standards anyway. They were still tight to show every bulge, but enough material hid the cracks.

She was a hard-looking woman, a been-around-the-block kind of woman who wore too much makeup to hide her age. He guessed she was over forty, looked fifty, and pretended to be thirty. Her hair she bleached one too many times. It resembled stiff straw and did little to enhance her appearance. He almost felt sorry for her.

Almost.

She sashayed to the bench with an exaggerated sway and sat down. She took an inordinate amount of time doing it, too.

"Now that you spent the night and hopefully not entirely in the bedroom," she said, "I assume you did a thorough search?"

His partner had conducted a search the day they went to the beach. Alena never mentioned the intrusion, but he did see a new chain-lock on the door. Just as well. Donovan was getting impatient; Odessa was getting impatient. His instincts said Alena didn't have the card. What he believed mattered little where money was involved.

Sam folded up his newspaper and placed it on the bench. He looked out across the lake, avoiding eye contact with Odessa. "It's not there," he said. "I looked the best I could for a card she can hide anywhere. Nothing. She doesn't have it."

"Did you check the lining in her purse?"

"I checked the lining of everything. It's not there."

Odessa stared down at her pointed shoes with a frown. "She's gotta have it, Sammie. If it's not in her apartment, then she's hiding it in the hospital."

He grunted. "Good luck with that. If it wasn't in her office, it could be anywhere." He looked at her.

"She doesn't have it, Odessa. What woman in her right mind will save porn shots of her fiancé with another woman? The man up and left her while she was comatose. She can't feel loyalty toward him. If she had the card, I'm certain she'd throw it at you without hesitation."

They watched two female joggers pass. Odessa stared at their asses far longer than Sam did. He wouldn't be a bit surprised to discover women as part of her clientele.

"What about the bank?" she asked. "Did you check for a safe deposit box?"

"No box."

"And the money?"

Sam sat forward with his elbows on his knees before answering. "His bank account hasn't been touched in two years. If he doesn't show up soon, the cash will go to the state's unclaimed property bureau. I stopped the transfer for now." He paused for effect. "Unless you happen to know where he is."

She ignored the comment. "Half of the four million is mine."

Sam sat back and stared. "Who says?"

"Johnny. Before he disappeared."

"Well, you'll be hard pressed proving that. No one will hand over two million bucks without sufficient documentation even to a woman who claims to be his *mother*." He leaned toward her with a wry grin on his lips.

She grinned back, equally wry. Sam swore her make-up would crack.

"He could have another bank," she said.

"I checked."

A bird landed near them. It took one look at Odessa and flew away.

"Did you find anything in Johnny's stuff, *mother*?"

"Junk mainly. Quite a few pictures of Johnny and Alena. What is it with this woman that men like to take photos of her all the time?" She eyed him with suspicion.

Sam sneered. "Yes, I know. You saw the photos in my place."

"They're surveillance photos, Sammie. What aren't you telling me?"

"Dave needed to know who she was, that's all. I gave him copies and kept a few for myself. Nice photos, don't you think?"

She grunted while adjusting her boobs.

"What else did you find?"

"Nothing to tell me anything," she complained. "No keys, no baggage claims, nothing. I can't figure out what he did with it."

"Except take it with him." Sam said. He hoped for a reaction. She did react. Her brown eyes glazed over as she stared at the lake.

"Were you jealous?" Sam asked.

Odessa looked at him. "Of what?"

"John and Alena. Their engagement."

"Ha!" She pulled on a skirt that was about to show her private parts. "I run a business, Sam McCullen. A very profitable business. Johnny was a steady customer but not my only one."

A hard fact to ignore. The influx of men in and out of her apartment aggravated the neighbors. "It doesn't explain his promise to give you two million."

She cocked her head. "A weak moment, Sammie. I

want you to help me get it."

He shook his head. "No can do. That would be an embezzlement charge. I don't feel like going to prison for you." *She must believe I'm the biggest sap around.* "I think he's dead. No one leaves four million in the bank untouched."

She fussed with the straw on her head. No waves, no curls, nothing. Straight straw. A horse would have a feast.

"Regardless whether he is dead or alive, I want my money, and you, dearie, will help me. Otherwise, I tell the lovely doctor that you are as much a phony as Johnny."

His head snapped. The bitch one-upped him, and he didn't like it one damn bit. He peered at her. "Meaning?"

"Your résumé at the bank doesn't check out. You might have an MBA in finance, but that's all we found."

He should have known. She was a pro, and pros have their connections. Even worse, she revealed a security breach at the bank. Someone unauthorized checked his résumé. An unacceptable piece of news. "I'm beginning to admire you, Odessa. You have spies everywhere. I suppose you have them at the hospital as well?"

She glared at him through slits. "What makes you think I'd go through so much trouble?"

"Depends on what the memory card means to you. It could show up. Johnny could show up. Infinite possibilities. You might want to know right away." He looked at her. "You checked me out for a reason. Care to elaborate?"

She flashed a sly smile. If he was right, he already knew the answer.

"I need a new partner, Sammie. John Goodhart and I had a business of selling things."

"What kind of things?" he asked.

"Never mind for now. But in answer to your question, yes, I'm keeping tabs on the doctor at the hospital. Joe is, in particular. He's in a great position being in security and all."

"He's a little young for you, don't you think?"

"Oh, he's returning a favor for a few life lessons. You don't have to worry, Sammie. I like my men with meat on their bones. Like you. Joe's not quite a man yet if you know what I mean. His sexual techniques are a bit awkward to say the least. The poor boy couldn't even get it in without a little help. I doubt I could say that about you. You look like the type who could satisfy a woman."

He'd never want to prove it with her though. There was one woman on his mind, and no one else would do.

"Maybe Joe should be your new business partner," he said. "I doubt I'll be interested. You can train him like a puppy." He faced her. "You can't blackmail me, Odessa."

"Maybe not, but you falsified your resume for a reason. All I have to do is figure out why."

They sat in silence for a few minutes to allow a group of elderly walkers to pass. Sam took the opportunity to scan for Alena in case she slipped by Dave. If she saw them sitting together, it would ruin everything. Bad enough he hadn't heard from her. She knew his feelings. What she did about it was up to her.

"What if we can't find the card, Odessa? What

would you do then?"

"I have to find it. It's worth an awful lot of money."

"For porn shots?"

She watched him. "When we become business partners, I'll explain. For now, porn shots."

Yeah, real convincing. He stared at the lake. "She is not to be harmed, Odessa." He met her gaze. "I mean that."

She laughed, a cruel, harsh laugh that echoed from the witch within. Her face turned serious. "Find the card so I can move away from this shithole. You'll be doing the doctor a favor. As for the money, work on it. If you succeed, I'll know you're worthy of a partnership." She stood to her feet. "For the record, Johnny and I made a lot of money. That should give you an incentive to be a good boy and do as you're told."

He stood also. "Speaking of favors, I believe you owe me some money. We made a deal, if you remember."

Her gaze scanned him from head to toe, resting a little longer than appropriate on his trouser zipper. A pair of polished red lips pursed in the process. "Stop by before the pretty doctor gets home. I'll give you a partial payment."

With a wink, she turned and wiggled her ass as she started up the path.

For a fact, her partial payment would not include money.

****

Alena stared down at her food tray and wondered why she bothered. She wasn't hungry. She hadn't been

167

hungry for several days now, but Nan said to meet for lunch. So, they met for lunch. They picked a secluded corner in the doctor's cafeteria away from the television on the wall. She didn't care if the world was ready to implode. Her life had reached another impasse. The end of the world would solve her problem.

Alena picked up a fork and stabbed her pudding.

"We definitely have a commitment problem," Nan said with a mouthful of food. "Usually, the man can't commit to a relationship. This time, it's us. Somewhere in our genetic make-up, we were cast from the same mold. I don't want to get involved with Nathan, and you don't want to get involved with Sam. We're weird." Alena responded with silence so Nan leaned forward on the table. "You need to talk, honey. You can't go moping around forever."

Finished with the pudding massacre, Alena started on the mashed potatoes. She now had pudding mixed into her potatoes. "I hurt Sam," she murmured.

"He'll get over you."

Alena's head snapped. "I don't want him to get over me!"

"He asked for friendship. You asked for friendship. He reneged on the agreement and fell in love. It's his problem." She struggled to cut her meat. She studied her knife to see if it had any semblance of an edge. "Maybe you fell in love, too."

"No."

"Are you sure? Your whole face glows when he's near you. Everyone saw it at the ball. I already knew Sam was in love with you."

"You did not!"

"Sorry, honey, but it shows in his eyes whenever

he looks at you. You kept your mind closed to the possibility."

Alena had seen the look in Sam's eyes. He had fallen in love too early in their friendship. She'd ignored it along with her own growing feelings. Every day, she had struggled with the possibility of a relationship. *What is wrong with you, girl?*

Sam had accused her of holding onto Johnny's memory. Why the hell should she? Johnny had upped and left her, dammit! She could be dead for all he cared. No, their last night together preyed on her mind. She couldn't shake the memory. Her heart admitted to the over-exaggeration of rape, but the experience of lying there like a vegetable and not giving back was hard to erase.

"Hey! You still with me?"

Alena jerked. "Sorry. Mind's wandering."

Nan borrowed Alena's knife but still had trouble cutting her meat. She glared at it. "Why can't we get edible meat in this damn cafeteria?"

She tried again, giving it her best shot, then gave up. She threw down the knife with defeat. "I guess they want us to go vegetarian. Tough meat, dull knifes. Can I have your pudding?" She grabbed Alena's pudding cup. She did a double-take at the mess and shot Alena a quizzical look. She ate it anyway. "The question is what now? You've got to start living one of these days. You know, sex, love, the relationship thing. At least Sam got you started."

"No, never again."

"Suit yourself." She returned the empty pudding cup to Alena's tray and searched for something else to grab. Finding nothing good, she sat back and picked up her own apple. "I suppose you can lock yourself in a hole somewhere with all your little hang-ups for company."

Alena gave her friend a severe glare. "My hang-ups are medically explained."

"Oh, bullshit!" Nan bit into her apple. "You use that cane as a reminder of a man who didn't have the courage to stick around when you needed him most. You ditch the cane, and you ditch his memory."

"That's ridiculous."

"Is it? Then tell me why you won't strengthen your leg? That is the one last part of your stroke to defeat."

Alena studied her friend, all smug and confident while munching on her apple. They had this conversation many times over the past year. Nan meant well, but Alena had always resisted her friend's efforts. Something told her she would have a difficult time resisting this one. She had no argument.

"You never gave me an answer before, and I don't expect to hear one now," Nan said. "Well, I'll tell you why. It's because your fear of another stroke during intercourse is your biggest hang-up of all. You keep the cane, you remind yourself of your leg weakness, and you avoid a relationship. A cycle you travel over and over." She put one foot up on her chair. "You can strengthen your leg, Alena, but I don't know what you can do about your head." She bit into her apple a little too deep. She spit out a seed.

Not to be outdone, Alena fired back. "You're a fine one to lecture me. You said Nathan reminds you of your father. I don't see that at all."

Nan stopped chewing. "You never met my father."

"Of course I never met your father, but your father

was an uneducated man. Nathan is obviously educated."

Nan grunted. "He can't be that educated if he's a janitor."

She threw her apple core onto the tray and foraged for more. "I'm still hungry."

Nan was always hungry. Everything she ate burned off faster than wood in a stove.

"At least Nathan has a job," Alena said. "That is so unlike your father. Give Nathan credit for that." She leaned forward on the table. "Yes, we both have hang-ups so don't lecture me about mine."

Nan made a face. "I hate logic."

Alena pushed her tray aside and sat back.

"I realize you're trying to help me. I like Sam, but he wants marriage. I've been down that road. He already said he would return to California. It's all a matter of when."

She crumbled her napkin into a ball and tossed it onto her tray.

"You might like California," Nan said.

Yeah, with all its mudslides, forest fires, and earthquakes. "I'll think about it."

"Well, don't think too long. He might find someone else in the meantime. Can you handle *that*?" Nan reached across the table and took Alena's hand. "I want to see you happy again, honey. Sam pulled you out of your shell, but you keep fighting to go back in. The man loves you. That's a hell of an incentive."

She patted Alena's hand then stood to her feet.

"I've got to get back to the ER. The nurses ordered pizza, and I want a slice." She picked up her tray and looked down at her friend with affection. "Don't let

Sam wait too long. The man deserves a good woman. If you don't want him, you've got to let him know. It's only fair."

Alena hated logic, too.

Chapter Twenty-One

Stretch, pull, lift.

Alena pushed, she pulled. She did everything as ordered, building up a sweat that made her look like a running faucet. She never knew getting back into shape would be so torturous.

She had gone through this grueling routine once before. This time, it wasn't for a paralysis. She was here to put Johnny to rest. She had to force herself into the world of the living. She wanted it to be with Sam. More than anything, with Sam…if he still wanted her.

The last exercise got her puffing. Alena grabbed a towel to wipe her face and neck before downing a half bottle of water.

A woman walked toward her. Sauntered was a good word, swaying her hips like a seesaw without kids. It drew every eye in the club, male and female alike. Alena puzzled over the familiarity of the body until the tight clothes triggered a memory of a scene in the parking lot, a scene with Sam and big breasts and no underwear. This was Odessa, the complex slut. The woman put every male in heat as she passed.

"So, you're Sammie's friend," Odessa said. She eyed Alena with venom.

Odessa was a shrewd-looking woman. Her eyes were half veiled by fake eyelashes too thick to show the color of the iris but not thick enough to hide the scrutiny. A too-small bra pushed her breasts above the line of her top showing fat and cellulite in the process. She obviously wasn't here to exercise. The slightest bend would rip every seam on her clothing.

Alena eyed her in turn, not in the least willing to give the bitch an edge. "And you must be Odessa," she said with equal disdain. "Are you following me?"

Her red lips twisted into a sneer. "Let's say I won't let you out of my sight. You have something I want, and I intend to get it."

The salt and peppered hair man. Of course. She hadn't seen him in the lobby for a while, but he must be there somewhere watching her. Unless a new man was in place.

Like Joe.

She inwardly gasped. Was Joe heading to Odessa's apartment that day? It made sense. Silly of her not to think of it sooner. How many more men did the woman have wrapped around her finger?

"I don't have the memory card, Odessa, but you already know that since one of your cronies did a thorough search of my place." The day she and Sam went to Cape May in fact. It had unnerved her to sense the violation of her privacy again. The next day, she'd made a quick run to the hardware store to buy a chain for the door. She didn't want them barging in while she slept. She never told Sam. As before, nothing was missing.

How could Johnny get involved with such a woman? She was at least fifteen years older with a face that passed through a wringer. She used a ton of make-up to hide the hard lines, and her hair—dear Lord! The best conditioner on the market couldn't help that hair.

She needed to shave it off and start over.

"What do you want, Odessa?"

"You know what I want. Just because you claim not to have it doesn't mean you don't. The hospital is loaded with hiding places. Why don't you save yourself trouble and hand it over? I'll pay good money for it."

Alena threw her towel onto the bench behind her. "Go find Johnny. He'll tell you where he hid it." He should have shoved it up Odessa's ass. "What makes you think he left it with me?"

"A logical assumption."

"Not really. Porn shots of you and him would terminate our engagement. He probably destroyed it."

"I don't think so, sweetie. He may have been stupid enough to fall in love with you, but he wasn't stupid enough to destroy something so valuable."

"Valuable? Aren't you giving yourself too much credit?"

The bitch sneered. "Johnny was a nice little puppet. He obeyed orders. Now, it's Sammie's turn. I like my men to follow orders, in the bedroom and out. Sammie's in training so it might take time, but he'll come around. They always do." She watched a man lifting weights on a bench press. Her eyes glowed at the sweat accumulating on his chest. "This is way too much work, honey. You should do what I do for exercise. It's more enjoyable." Her eyes turned into slits. "Find the card, doctor, and find it quickly. My patience is wearing thin." She turned away.

"Why? What makes this card so important when you already have porn shots posted all over the web?"

The woman turned back. "That's my business, dearie. Find the card so I can get the hell out of your life." She leaned close. "And I plan on taking Sammie with me." She swaggered away.

Was it Odessa's mission in life to steal every man from her? What power did she have...

Oh, get real.

Sex was the woman's weapon. Rough sex and plenty of it. Alena refused to believe that Sam slept with such a witch. She still couldn't believe it about Johnny. Yet, watching Odessa wiggle away made her more determined than ever to defeat the woman at her own game. Alena would fight tooth and nail if necessary to take Sam McCullen as her own.

And with that thought...

Sam said to call if anyone approached. She hadn't talked to Sam since the morning in her living room. She wasn't about to call him now because Odessa showed up. She had special plans for Sam, and she didn't want to spoil it by calling too soon. He knew about Odessa. He knew about the memory card. He didn't know that Alena Nichols was determined to put her stroke behind her.

A sense of foreboding hit. There was more going on with Johnny than porn shots of two lovers in bed. Every fiber in her body said so. But what, dammit? And how deep was Sam in all of this?

The answers were in the memory card.

****

Sam leaned against his car waiting for a certain blue sedan to pull into the complex parking lot. She had left the fitness club forty minutes ago. He hoped she didn't stop anywhere. He was already boiling mad. The longer she took, the hotter he got. An extended delay could trigger an explosion.

After a lifetime, the car pulled into its assigned slot. He strolled over, forcing himself to stay calm, stay focused as Odessa stepped out. Her red lips broke into a wicked sneer. "Hi, Sammie. Coming over for your payment?"

"You weren't to approach her, Odessa."

"Well, well. She called you, I assume. You never said anything about approaching her. You said not to harm her, which I didn't. It was with a crowd of people so you shouldn't get upset."

He wasn't upset. He was livid. "I'm trying to find the card for you. It won't help matters if you spook her."

Odessa snickered. "She's not easily spooked, Sammie. She's cool and level-headed, my kind of woman."

Sam shuddered at the comparison. Alena might be cool and levelheaded, but she wasn't a cold-blooded killer. Nor was she a pro who lived by her own set of rules. Odessa was trash, plain and simple. "I don't want you near her."

"Or what? You going to spank me?" She wiggled her ass.

No, he wanted to break her nose and align it with her wrinkles.

"I need that card, Sammie. Time's running out. I've got a buyer who's willing to pay an exorbitant amount of money for it."

"You may have to tell him to take a hike. I don't know where it is. I don't think anyone does. You're playing with fire by promising delivery for something you don't have."

She leaned toward him, her posture threatening.

"Don't tell me how to run my business. That's the first lesson you learn when you work for me. The second lesson is to accommodate. So, you and I are going into my place and strip. I could use a little rough sex after my trip to the fitness club. Watching those hunky men work out put me in heat."

Rough sex? Yeah, with his hands around her throat.

"Sorry, Odessa. I haven't agreed to a partnership yet. If and when I do, then you can order me around. For now, it's the card. I'll find it. I don't know how nor do I know when, but if you frighten Alena, she could run to the cops. After that, you may as well kiss your card goodbye." He leaned toward her. "As for my payment, I'll collect when I hand over the card."

He turned on his heel and walked away.

Chapter Twenty-Two

Sam listened with patience to the long dissertation from the man on the other end of his phone. He hated doing business at home. He especially hated to do it on a Friday evening, but he was a bank president. Bank presidents got phone calls at all hours.

This phone call was from a major suckass who had latched onto Sam before the big man sat in his office chair. Zach wanted to move up the ladder and believed Sam McCullen could catapult his dream. Little did Zach know he sucked up to a temporary president, a man who would say adios once the job reached its conclusion.

"Can't blame you there, Zach. I agree one hundred percent."

Bad enough the man bored him to death. He agreed to no clue what.

He hadn't been honest with Alena. He had fed her lies from the beginning, a practiced art that went with the job. She deserved to know the truth about everything. Hell, he'd proposed marriage. He shouldn't have, but he wanted her in his life—if she accepted his 'life'. His ex-wife didn't.

"Who are you talking about, Zach? Yeah? No kidding!"

Not like he gave a damn. Zach could say anything he wanted because Sam's mind stayed on Alena. He

179

thought of her every hour of the day. Three weeks had passed without a word, a note, nothing. He forced himself to stay off the balcony in the morning until she left. She arrived home after dark every evening. He'd kept his eye on her anyway—as did everyone else. Alena Nichols was the key to this entire mystery. Without the key, they had nothing.

"What's that, Zach?" The guy asked one question after another of which he heard none. "Sorry. My mind's wandering. Repeat what you said."

He should never have fallen in love. This was a job like all the others, and he was a trained professional. To do the job right, it required travel, a fact his ex-wife never understood. Some trips, like this one, took months.

Alena might not understand the trips either.

Why hadn't he steeled himself better? All right, yes, she was beautiful, but beautiful women were part of California living. He knew what Alena looked like before he arrived. Up close, though, she had taken his breath away, but to fall in love was asinine. Like a fool, he allowed his feelings to override his common sense. What made her so special when so many jobs involved breathtaking women?

He had tormented himself for months over that last question. He'd fallen for Alena Nichols hard. Her eyes, her mouth, her smile. Everything about her. All his senses had come alive when they were together. He loved it when they touched. Even the slightest brush against her sent him reeling.

What was a man to do when a woman wasn't willing? He would never force her, but he wanted to taste more than her lips. She had to come to him. She had to let that bastard fiancé go and allow herself to love again.

Yeah, listen to yourself. You're suddenly a therapist.

"No, I don't think so, Zach. Check with accounting on Monday."

He'd almost stopped for a mushroom pizza before coming home tonight. He debated and again thought of Alena. They had sat at that restaurant table and evened out the mushrooms on every slice until she popped a few into her mouth. He caught her and popped a few of his own. Boy, did they laugh!

"I don't think it's so funny," Zach complained.

Oops. Wandering again. Easy enough to do with this guy's mundane voice. "Sorry, Zach, my concentration is somewhere else."

"We could meet at a bar. I know a place where some well-endowed women hang out—literally. Maybe that's what you need."

That was what he needed all right instead of waiting for a woman who might never show. But not with Zach. The man had no life outside of his job.

Just like Sam McCullen.

He should thank his ex-wife for that amazing revelation.

"It's a tempting offer, but right now, I want to put my feet up and relax."

"No better way to relax, man."

Performing for a stranger was not his definition of relaxation. "Another time, Zach. I'll talk to you next week." He ended the call and threw the phone onto the kitchen counter. The last thing he wanted was to screw a woman who made it a habit of screwing other men.

Like Odessa.

His phone chirped. A text message. He read quickly. *Bidding on a roll. Seven figures and counting. Extra eyes authorized.*

The bidding was for a missing memory card. Seven figures. Too high, too high. Greed increased desperation. Alena was in danger now, far more than she ever was. He didn't like the news one damn bit. He again threw the phone on the counter.

Shit, what a dilemma. She needed to know. She needed to watch her back, look around, and be aware. Alena also needed to know what he really did for a living. If anything ever happened to her, he would never forgive himself. He flopped onto the sofa, threw his head back on the cushion, and closed his eyes.

He and Alena weren't talking. He needed to reestablish communication somehow. Her life was worthless to so many, the very life she struggled to regain after her stroke. The indecision was ripping his gut apart.

Someone ran up his staircase. He opened his eyes to glare at the door, daring that person to knock. A few seconds later, that someone ran down again.

Someone again ran up. Was this about to go on all night? Ah, but this time, no return flight down. The inevitable knock on the door. He debated answering. He debated too long, and the knock sounded again. Not in the mood for a sales call, he charged for the door with a snarl. He threw it open.

Alena stood there looking tanned and beautiful in tank top and shorts. He blinked.

"That was *you* running up my stairs?"

"Yeah." She gave him a shy half-grin. "Can I talk

to you?"

Hell, yes! She could talk. She could yell. She could beat him to a pulp. Whatever she wanted. He didn't care, but he acted nonchalant as one friend to another. What he hoped she would say and what she might say flashed through his mind faster than a microchip. He ushered her in. "Have a seat."

"No—thanks. I can't sit…yet. I only want to talk to you."

Sam sat on a kitchen stool. "Okay, talk."

She was nervous as hell. She paced. She wrung her hands. Her sandy eyes darted here and there, focusing on nothing. Not a part of her stood still. Sam waited and watched, enjoying her presence in his living room. He especially enjoyed the unrestrained breasts beneath the tank top. An absolute feast for his eyes.

And no cane!

"You ran up my stairs!" he repeated with genuine surprise.

"Yes." She flashed him a nervous grin. "I've been doing intense physical therapy for two weeks now. My trainer told me to expect periods of weakness, but for the most part, I can do without my cane."

He had known where she went every night after work. She never went anywhere without him receiving a detailed report of where she was, who she was with, and what she was doing. That's how he knew Odessa approached her. Big deal, he had gotten a report that she exercised at a fitness club. No one told him how hard.

"I'm proud of you, Alena."

More than proud. He wanted to cry. He wanted to hold her, hug her, and shout with joy. At long last, she worked to put her stroke behind her. "Is this what you wanted to talk about?"

"Yes—no! Bear with me, Sam." She paced like a performer about to enter center stage for the first time. She turned. "Am I keeping you from anything?"

"I would cancel a trip around the world for you, Alena."

This relaxed her, and she grinned. "No, you wouldn't."

He gasped. "You doubt my word?"

The grin faded. The nervous expression returned. "No, I don't." She watched him. He watched her back. "Would you answer one question with complete honesty? I mean it, Sam. I need to know."

"All right. Shoot."

She bit her lower lip, her gaze uncertain. "Did you sleep with Odessa?"

He studied her. "What do you believe?"

"My heart says no, you didn't."

"Your heart tells you correctly. There is only one woman I want to sleep with, and she's standing in my living room right now."

At least she didn't bolt. That was hopeful.

"I've been holding back telling you this, Sam…no, let me talk. I fell in love with you early in our friendship. I think it was when you showed up with the bowtie and cummerbund in your hand." The pacing resumed. "I kept quiet about it because we agreed to be friends. Your divorce and my stroke erected barriers that stood like a safety zone. I wanted to stay in that zone for a while because I wasn't ready for you or any man." She stole a glance at him. "A relationship meant sexual intercourse, and the thought terrified me." She stopped in front of the double doors to the balcony and stared out.

"I had a good talk with myself about you." She faced him. "I realized my feelings go far deeper for you than they ever did for Johnny. So much love flowed through your lips that morning. It awakened every dormant hormone in my body."

"I felt the love in your lips, too."

Her mouth fell open. "You did?"

"Lips don't lie."

She nodded then took a slow, deep breath. Her pale eyes stayed glued to his face. "I'm willing to take a chance with you, Sam."

"I meant what I said, Alena. I want all of you, and you better be ready because I intend to lay it on hot and heavy."

She swallowed hard. "I'm ready—if you still want me."

Want her? His heart exploded with the words. He wanted to hold her, kiss her, and love her forever. He struggled with the overwhelming conflict that rose from deep within. She knew nothing about the real Sam McCullen. What should he say? When should he tell her?

Friggin' rules. Always the friggin' rules.

"Come over here," he said.

Alena stepped toward him. He grabbed her with more force than he intended, and his hands searched for skin to hold. Without hesitation, he slipped her tank top over her head to expose her chest to his eyes. He choked on a sob at the sight of her breasts. So beautiful. Round, soft. Their lips met and fused together. Her kiss responded to the heat of his own with a fierceness that pushed him over the edge.

She tasted wonderful. There was a cherry flavor on her lips that got his tongue probing for more. Then she rubbed against him in a way only a woman could do, and his hormones flew into a rage. He lifted her in his arms and carried her to the bedroom.

Fear lurked in the desert sand. She couldn't hide it. Sam believed this a make-or-break trial, one that could drive her to ecstasy or push her back into a shell. If ever a woman tested his skill as a man, this woman was it.

He eased her down on the bed and slipped alongside, every movement slow and deliberate. He touched her chin, in no hurry to rush into an activity that still caused fear.

"Let me get a few things straight before we continue," he said. "I am not John Goodhart. I am Sam McCullen, a man who loves you very much, a man who wants to strip you naked and make love to you day and night. You are the woman who restored my faith in the female sex, the one who made me feel love again after my ex-wife tore my heart into shreds. Your willingness to be here fills me with a profound happiness. Together, we will erase your fear forever."

Her lips separated to speak, but he silenced them with his finger.

"You must know that I am yours through thick or thin no matter what life throws at us. I love you so much, Alena. You are the reality I need in my life, and I don't ever want it to change. Do you understand?"

He kissed her hard with a greed she returned in kind. His tongue explored every square inch of her mouth, her cheeks, ears, eyes. Not satisfied yet, his lips traveled down her neck to the soft breasts. He wanted to rip the rest of her clothes off, but he fingered the waistband to her shorts instead, brushing his finger across her belly, teasing her but tormenting himself. He kissed her waist, higher, still higher until his lips suckled the hard nipple on her breast. Unable to hold off any longer, he removed her clothing.

A beauty. No doubt about it. She was a dream come true. *God help me to be patient.*

"You take my breath away," he whispered as his gaze took her in. "Do you have any plans for the weekend?"

"Just you."

He damned near ripped off his own clothes.

Tears welled in his eyes. The emotional release for this woman gushed everything to the surface. He loved the feel of her smooth skin, the scent of an intoxicating perfume, the taste of her mouth and then her breasts, round and delicious. Real breasts, not the LA implants.

He loved this woman. He had questioned his sanity because of her. He'd questioned his purpose on the east coast, the importance of the memory card, his job, hell, his entire life. Alena Nichols was the most important being in the world. Everything else was insignificant. He would die for her if necessary.

The moist heat between her legs shattered his thoughts. His fingers worked their magic. He bit her hard nipples.

"Sam!"

No fear in that voice. He recognized the plea of a woman tethering on the edge. But not yet. As anxious as he was, this moment had to last a bit longer. He suckled her breast, flicking the nipple with his tongue. To the other one. A feast for his mouth, a banquet for his eyes.

"Sammie, please!"

"Ah, my dear, a condom first."

"Agggh!"

"Patience, sweetheart, patience."

His hands shook. Anxiety, excitement, anticipation. A slew of words surfaced. Ready, he smiled down at her as he cast her in shadows. With a thrust, he sent her to the moon.

Chapter Twenty-Three

The fear was gone. She wanted Sam, wanted all of him with the power only a man could give. He gave with force, with gentleness, and with a love that brought her to tears.

His rough hands caressed her skin, slowly and non-stop, causing a stimulus that raised goosebumps. His mouth tasted her breasts while his hot breath stimulated the nipple into a hard protrusion that tempted his teeth. He bit and nibbled as his hand continued to travel until slipping into the moist heat between her legs. She wanted to reciprocate and explore his body, but he held her hands overhead, leaving her nakedness for him to enjoy.

She couldn't speak. He wouldn't let her. Every time she opened her mouth, he smothered it with his own. He hovered over her, his eyes dark with a flame that ignited her soul. Time and again, he thrust deep within her, using the power of his size and strength to tantalize until a climax shook her core. When a cry escaped from her throat, his release exploded within her. She had never experienced anything so wonderful.

Was her love for Johnny real? Sam's lovemaking raised doubts. Somewhere in the back of her brain, Alena had believed the stroke destroyed her emotions. Sam proved her wrong. A love poured out of her with every touch, her greed for him insatiable. Was her stroke a godsend instead of a curse?

It had taken two years to feel again, and Sam was the cure.

Hours later, they snuggled side-by-side, hot and sweaty. She touched his cheek. He took her hand and kissed it.

"I'm still here," she whispered with a slight sob. No stroke, no flaccid body, just sated and happy. He smiled as he captured her mouth.

"I love you, Sam."

"I know," he whispered. "I always knew."

He bit her lower lip while a hand cupped her breast. His thumb pressed the hard nipple. "I'm not letting you leave here," he whispered.

She couldn't think of a better way to spend a weekend.

Alena woke mid-morning to the smell of coffee. The happiness generated by a night with Sam filled her with a determination to try anything. Her stroke was behind her. Her feelings of rape and desertion smashed into oblivion because of this one gentle giant.

She wiped away the tears streaming down her cheeks. Tears of happiness. She reached for the nightstand drawer and opened it.

She jerked back with a gasp.

A large photograph met her wide-eyed stare. She took it out of the drawer to discover more underneath. They were covert photos, taken as she exited the hospital, her apartment, her car. Sam had followed her. The question was why? Was he working with Odessa? Was their night together all a game?

Scenarios flashed through her mind faster than lightning. What if Odessa had succeeded in wrapping

Sam around her finger? She was a pro. She had the skills to manipulate, to coerce…to blackmail.

That was the answer. Sam was a bank president. Odessa had uncovered something to blackmail him and destroy his career. What could it be?

Alena needed to know. She moved to jump out of bed when she looked up and froze. Sam blocked the doorway. A chill traveled her spine from the hard expression in his gaze.

"I was searching for a tissue," she explained. "I keep mine in the nightstand drawer, and I opened it without thinking. I—huh…why do you have these?"

He stood in stone silence. His chest and feet were bare, but he had on his trousers. He studied her, his eyes scrutinizing, analyzing…dissecting. It proved unnerving, and she grabbed the bed sheet to cover her nakedness.

Sam reached into his back trouser pocket and took out a black billfold. He tossed it on the bed. "Look at that."

She expected a horse whipping not further instructions. She took the billfold and opened it, half-afraid the leather would explode in her face.

Again, she jerked back with a gasp. "You work for the U.S. Treasury?"

He nodded, his face stoic and hard. "Get dressed, and I'll explain everything while we eat."

Eat? He expected her to eat?

For several long minutes, she stared at the ID badge in her hand.

Samuel B. McCullen, Special Agent
U.S. Treasury, California Bureau
Why the charade? Why her?

She couldn't get her clothes on fast enough.

Alena sat at the kitchen counter and watched him prepare breakfast. He slipped on a shirt but left it unbuttoned. Neither one of them spoke. She was curious as hell. Her mind raced, her thoughts colliding and turning her questions into a jumbled lump. After placing food and coffee on the counter, he sat next to her. His face relaxed somewhat to reveal the man she knew. She kept her questions to herself and waited.

"I want you to eat something first," he said.

She tasted the scrambled eggs and realized she was famished. Yes, she could eat after all.

He poured coffee into their cups. "A little over two years ago," he began, "the database at the California bureau of the U.S. Treasury was downloaded by an employee in our IT department. By the time we identified the thief, he had sold the database to a buyer in Las Vegas. The buyer was a fence, someone who buys the goods then sells to the highest bidder. We caught the employee easily enough, and he is now in a federal penitentiary. The fence got away. Vegas, being Vegas, had cameras everywhere so it didn't take long to identify the fence. We followed him from the casino to the airport. We followed him when he landed and then ultimately to you." He faced her. "The fence was John Goodhart."

Alena choked on her eggs. She coughed and sputtered before dropping her fork with a clang. She stared, awe-struck.

"You okay?" he asked.

"Yes. Go on."

Sam helped himself to more bacon before continuing. "By the time we pieced the facts together,

John Goodhart went missing. The Vegas videos showed him with a female accomplice whom we had yet to identify so we kept you on surveillance in case he showed up. He never did. You were in the hospital, and we confirmed that he visited twice before you went into surgery. After that, he disappeared." Sam poured cream into his coffee.

"Sam, I—"

He put a finger to her lips. "Let me continue." He sipped his coffee. "I took an undercover position at the bank where Johnny kept his money. We assumed his female accomplice would try to access it. We assumed wrong, of course. I then moved to this complex strategically positioned to watch your apartment. The accomplice in the Vegas videos always wore a large, floppy hat so we were unable to track her down. I knew in my heart it wasn't you. When we found Johnny, my belief was substantiated."

She turned on her stool, wide-eyed. "You found Johnny?"

He watched her, his eyes probing to her soul. "Johnny didn't abandon you, Alena. We found him with a bullet hole in his head off the Atlantic City Expressway. The medical examiner estimated his death at approximately two years ago. It was a dumpsite. We have yet to find his car. It's possible that it went straight into a chop shop."

She went mute, staring in disbelief. A cold shiver lifted her hair ends.

Sam sipped his coffee and continued. "Johnny's time of death cleared you. We knew he was alive at the time of your stroke because of security footage at the hospital. We then concentrated on the second female in our sights, the one who cleaned out his locker, his office, and his apartment."

Her mouth fell open. "Odessa!"

"Correct, Odessa. When you told me about your furnishings being trashed, we compared the Vegas videos to the storage videos and saw some similarities." He chuckled. "We did an ass comparison. When we included Odessa's photo, we got a match. After she approached me with that cockamamie story about photos on the memory card, I knew for certain that she was Johnny's accomplice. She wants that database and has no idea where Johnny hid it. She assumes—as do we—that you have it."

"But—"

He again silenced her with his finger. This time he traced along her jaw line before continuing. "I know you don't have it, but Odessa will never believe it. The bid is high for the information on that card, and Odessa wants it. Your life is in danger now." He finished his coffee and stared into his empty cup.

All this information sounded impossible. She remembered Johnny's trip to Vegas. For a conference, he said. Not long after his return, her stroke hit. He'd led the federal agents straight to her door, and she hadn't a clue about any of it.

"What now?" she asked with hesitation. She expected his finger against her lips again.

He gave her a half-grin then leaned over to kiss her. His lips revealed tenderness, but she had trouble responding. Too many unanswered questions.

"The memory card is paramount," he said. "I need to find it before Odessa."

A miracle in the making, Alena mused. Then a

scene with Johnny and a gun to his head flashed through her mind. He never abandoned her. A bullet took him instead. She shuddered.

"Did Odessa kill Johnny?" she asked.

Sam met her gaze. "That's hard to say. Why would she kill the one man who hid the memory card? Johnny's body revealed evidence of torture before someone put a bullet in him. We suspect one of Odessa's men got a little too zealous. If the shooter acted independently of her command, then that someone might be six feet in the ground by now. We don't have a shred of proof either way. What we do suspect is that Johnny knew his days were numbered. We puzzled over the fact that he never tried to conceal his identity from the cameras on the casino floor. At one point, he actually looked up. Maybe he hoped to get caught."

When was Johnny going to tell her about his illegal activities? After their first born?

"Why Vegas, Sam? Everyone and their mother knows the city is loaded with cameras."

"It was the IT tech's suggestion. He was there on some kind of program upgrade course. A government requirement, of all things."

The irony in the statement didn't escape her. She pushed her half-eaten plate aside in disgust. "What about you, Sam?"

He cocked an eyebrow. "Meaning?"

"I seem to have a knack for falling in love with men who lead a double life. I'm having difficulty separating fact from fiction. All this time, I believed you to be a bank president."

He took her hand. "Then believe me when I tell

you that my love for you is real. I wasn't supposed to tell you any of this, but it became unavoidable. Trust me, I wrestled with the decision to tell you earlier. I fell in love with one of our suspects so I broke all the rules with this case."

"What about Johnny's father? Are you the reason he disappeared from my office?"

"One of our men recognized him entering the hospital. We had to get him away from you before he told you who came knocking at his door. We already knew hospital procedure concerning the fire alarm so they set it off. While you were closing doors, two of our men grabbed him."

"And your ex-wife?" She cringed. "Did you kill her?"

"No. She took her own life because I was about to lock her away. She came to expose me and blow this case wide open. We couldn't let that happen. While I was out in the hall on my phone, she threw the chair out the window. By the time I knocked down the door, she had already jumped. She wanted revenge, Alena. She blamed me for destroying our marriage and turning her into an addict."

Alena removed her hand from his. "If you're away for months at a time, then I understand how she felt. You can't have a happy marriage that way, Sam. You should never have fallen in love with me." And she with him when she thought about it.

She slipped off the stool and walked to the balcony doors. Yes, a straight line to her apartment. Not an obstruction in sight. His furnishings made sense, too. Everything looked like it came from a yard sale. Except the sofa. That looked decent.

"I suppose Odessa moved here to keep an eye on me, too," she said. Amazing. Everyone probably heard when she flushed the toilet. She moved away from the doors. "This means your stay on the east coast is temporary. At least that fact is clear." She faced him. "Why are you using your real name if you're under cover?"

"Because Sam McCullen really has an MBA in finance. If anyone went checking, that fact was certain. Remember, we had no idea who Johnny's partner was. A woman, yes, but did she work at the bank? Or was it the hospital?" He finished the last piece of bacon.

"The CEO at the bank knew my true purpose there," he continued, "and that was to keep an eye on Johnny's bank account along with a credible cover. You became my primary focus once we surmised that something drastic had happened to Johnny. When his body turned up, we knew we were right."

He slipped off the stool, took her hand, and guided her to the sofa. They sat down. "I have to find that memory card, Alena, and you're going to help me."

"Me! What am I supposed to do?"

"Well, we know the card wasn't in any of Johnny's belongings. Odessa made sure of that. She searched everything you owned while you were convalescing so the only logical place left is the hospital. Johnny used this one hospital, correct? Then it has to be in that building somewhere."

Her mouth fell open. "It's a 600 bed facility, Sam! How can you expect to search a place so large?"

"I can't. That's why I need your help. Maybe we can figure out where he hid it."

She fell back on the sofa cushions and ran her

fingers through her hair. This was like throwing a rock in the air and expecting it to hit a cloud. "You're asking the impossible. Johnny was an ear, nose, and throat specialist. He worked with the very young to the very old. He went everywhere in that hospital. I wouldn't know where to begin."

She dropped her hand and looked at him. "Maybe there's a key to a storage box at a train station. You see it all the time in the movies." She snapped her fingers. "How about his office? It's a large practice. He could have easily hidden something there." She sat forward but stopped when she caught his expression. "What?"

He sat smiling at her. "You're beautiful."

She made a face. "Don't get all mushy on me. I'm trying to help." She fell back against the cushions, feeling dejected.

Sam put his arm across the back of the sofa and caressed her hair. "We already searched his office, Alena. One of our agents was part of the cleaning service. He had all the time he needed for a thorough search." He toyed with a strand of her hair.

"For the record, you are doing this for your government, not for me. The information on that card could destroy this country."

Oh, hell. He would throw patriotism at her. She stood to her feet. "All right, we'll give it a try. I'll go home and change."

"Why?"

"I'm not going to the hospital looking like this!"

"We're not going today. I need to tell my boss our plans and arrange backup. Tomorrow is Sunday. We'll go then. I've got other plans for today." He swept her up into his arms and carried her into the bedroom.

"Did you ever put a condom on a man?" he asked. He placed her on the bed.

"I...umm, no."

He undressed her, his movements slow and deliberate. Then, he undressed himself. "It's high time you tried it, don't you think? You might enjoy it."

She peered at him. "I know *you* will." She cocked her head. "What if I take too long?"

He stretched out onto the bed, waiting. "Take as long as you want. We'll consider it foreplay."

Torture was the word. For her. She made damn sure for him, too.

Chapter Twenty-Four

After an entire night of lovemaking on Friday, then continuing into the better part of Saturday, Alena walked into the hospital on Sunday wobbly-kneed. She couldn't remember having such a wonderful weekend. Sam's lovemaking was extraordinary, so unlike Johnny's roll-over-and-die behavior. Sam had taken his time and relished her in a way no man had ever done. He made her feel special with every movement of his hand and every touch of his lips. She bolted to heaven and back with each penetration.

Unfortunately, the news about his job had weighed on her mind. His deception had haunted her, stifling the joy she'd felt earlier. She loved him, but a husband running off on an undercover assignment left a sick feeling in her heart. No amount of lovemaking had alleviated the feeling. She kept telling herself to enjoy the moment, enjoy him while he was here and in her life, however brief.

It didn't work. She fought off the misery it caused and lost. Even now as they walked into the hospital, gloom overwhelmed any apprehension about the memory card. She didn't give a horses' ass about finding it if it meant Sam leaving.

Alena guided Sam toward a staff elevator and punched the button for the radiology floor. "We'll start there," she said. "Johnny came often enough to see me and study x-rays, but radiology covers the entire floor, Sam. It might take all day for that one department." How the hell Sam expected them to look for an object so small in a place so large was beyond her comprehension.

"Doesn't matter. We have to start somewhere." Sam stopped the elevator and looked at the ceiling.

"No cameras," she assured.

He nodded his approval and took her by the shoulders. "Remember what we talked about. Odessa said the card contains photos of her and Johnny. That's all you know. You are to follow my instructions explicitly. Is that clear?"

"Yes, I understand."

They had a long discussion on the drive over. The less she revealed, the greater her safety. Odessa was a pro with dangerous connections. Sam's warning made perfect sense. He wanted no heroics from her, and she'd agreed. She wasn't the world's bravest person.

Still, the whole idea of searching a hospital was daunting. With Johnny being dead, it could be lost forever. They needed a clue, an epiphany, anything dammit. Hell, she'd settle for Johnny's ghost.

As they approached the x-ray reading room, furniture blocked their path. The furnishings from the reading room lined both sides of the hall.

"What's going on?" Sam asked with surprise.

"I think they're scrubbing and waxing the floor. I've complained about it for months. Hospitals do their patient areas daily, but when it comes to where the staff works, it's like pulling teeth to get it done."

They approached the doorway to see a young man in a blue uniform leaning against the doorjamb. Inside the room, an older man worked a floor scrubber. The young man turned. His eyes swept over her in two seconds flat.

"Dr. Nichols, you look *hot*!"

She wore a tee-shirt and blue jeans, rare attire for her within the hospital walls. "Thanks, Tommy. Looks like you two are doing a good job."

His face beamed. "It took us a while to get all the stuff out. Once we did, we scrubbed the walls. It needed it." He thumbed a hand gesture toward the man in the room. "Jack won't let me handle the floor scrubber yet. He said it requires a skilled hand." He rolled his eyes.

She scanned the room with approval. "It's going to look like a new room. Don't let me hold you up." She turned to Sam. "I'll start with the stuff in the hall. It's too tight for the two of us so we'll only get in each other's way. If you want, you can start in the conference room. Johnny gave a lot of lectures in there."

"Sounds good."

His cell phone chirped. A frown burrowed into his forehead as he read. "I'll use the restroom first. Where is it?"

"Down the hall on the left."

He turned and headed to the young man in the doorway instead. Sam asked a question. A surprised Tommy nodded. The frown on Sam's face deepened, and he shot her a look that raised her hair ends. He scratched his ear and headed to the restroom.

Alena jerked. The ear scratch was a prearranged signal. It meant 'be alert, act natural'. He had told her that eyes watched...good guys as well as bad. She fought the urge to look up at the camera mounted in the hall, but it didn't matter who watched. It didn't matter if

Tommy and his coworker were nearby. She never felt so utterly alone.

Tommy approached. "By the way, Dr. Nichols, we found a lot of junk behind the filing cabinets. Most of it we tossed, others I placed in a pile, but we also found this." He walked to one of the tables and picked up a dust-covered five by eight shipping envelope. He handed it to her. "Joe from security wanted to hold it for you, but I wouldn't let him leave the floor with it."

Her heart stopped. The return address was *John Goodhart's old apartment*!

The package had a two-year old postmark. Her gut twisted with realization. This was the memory card. It *had* to be. She searched the hall for Sam when her cell phone rang. She stared at the caller ID. Sam?

"Wait in the conference room," he commanded. "We're watching you, Alena."

The connection ended. Something was about to go down, and that was why Sam disappeared.

Oh, dear.

She studied the package in her hand and blew off the dust. A scrawled 'Personal—ER' was in red with ER crossed out and 'Radiology' written under it. Since other doctors handled her mail while she was convalescing, this one marked personal waited for her return. How did anyone know it was here except Tommy...and Joe.

She looked up at the camera at the end of the hall. Spies were everywhere, Sam said. The hospital security system. Of course. How easy. She followed Sam's order and walked into the conference room.

She paced, waiting, wondering with every nerve on edge. Where the hell was he? She wasn't trained for this covert activity. She was a doctor. She fixed people. She had no experience playing James Bond. Ready to scream, she turned to bolt from the conference room only to see a woman blocking the doorway.

Odessa!

Joe McMann stood behind her, acting more like a puppy than a security guard. Alena froze.

"I see it finally turned up," Odessa said with a cocky grin. She stepped into the room.

Alena looked at the package in her hand and stood her ground. "We don't know that for sure." She swallowed hard since the moisture in her throat turned to sand. "I haven't opened it yet."

"Best that you don't, sweetie." She swaggered into the room. "It's a good thing you didn't marry Johnny. He wasn't what he appeared."

No one was as they appeared these days. Johnny. Odessa. Sam. Now, Joe. And where the hell was Sam? "What are you doing here?"

"Joe called me. He saw the package. He guessed right, didn't he?" She glanced around the conference room. "Where's Sam by the way? He should have called, too."

"Bathroom. He doesn't know about the package."

The eyes that watched. Well, well. No wonder they couldn't find any paperwork for the extra cameras. There never was any. Joe was another of Odessa's puppets.

Alena scanned the perimeter of the ceiling. No cameras in here. She was on her own.

Act natural. Don't show you're afraid.

Famous last words. Alena threw her shoulders back. "You can kiss Sam when he comes out."

"I fully intend to, dearie. Do you know he is as big a phony as Johnny?"

Two could play this damn game. "What do you mean?"

"Sam is no more a bank president than you or I. He's stringing you along." Odessa's face changed to stone. "Give me the package."

"I'm going to open it first." Alena ripped at it before Odessa could protest. She needed one last chance to vindicate Johnny, to prove she fell in love with a good man, but she condemned him. The memory card dropped into her hand. She handed it to Odessa then slumped back against the conference table with disgust.

"Smart move, honey." Her eyes glowed with pure greed as she placed the card in her purse.

"Get out of here, Odessa. I don't ever want to see you again."

"Don't worry. You won't. Now that I have this—" She tapped her purse. "I can move out of that dumpy apartment." She turned on her heel and left the conference room. Joe hesitated.

"I'm sorry, Dr. Nichols."

Alena looked at him, a pitiful young man who couldn't quite fill out his clothes. "Your mistress left without you, Joe. Better run before she tugs on your leash." Alena flopped into a conference room chair, swallowing the nausea creeping up her esophagus. Relief rose with it. Her job was done. The rest was up to Sam and the U.S. Treasury. She could do nothing more but wait for Sam.

A commotion vibrated the walls. Men's voices, angry voices. A gunshot exploded above the noise.

Running footsteps. All this in a split second. Alena sat rigid in the chair, hands gripping the armrests, staring with frightened eyes at the open door. Sam said to stay put if gunfire arose. Should she at least hide under the table?

Too late. Odessa flew back into the room. With lightning speed, her arm slipped around Alena's neck, lifting her off the seat and pinning the chair between them. Cold metal pressed against her temple.

Uh-oh.

Two men charged into the room, weapons drawn. One man was Sam, looking angry as hell. The other was the man with the salt and pepper hair!

"Let her go, Odessa. You're finished!"

"Like hell! You have to let me out of here, or I'll put a bullet through her head!"

Was this how she was destined to die? Survive a stroke but die from a bullet to the brain?

She struggled. A fruitless effort. Odessa's arm tightened around her throat.

"Stay still, sweetie. You do as you're told, and you'll stay alive. You're my insurance policy."

"We're federal agents," Sam said through tight teeth. "Put down the gun. It's over."

Odessa's arm stiffened. Alena sensed the anger in that arm. A man playing an equally cunning game fooled the bitch.

Oh, dear. To hell with the bullet in her brain. Odessa was choking her to death!

Johnny, why did you do this to me? Wasn't my stroke enough?

Alena struggled to draw air into her lungs. She tried to kick her way out of the chair, but Odessa had the strength of a bull elephant. *Now what*?

"You hurt her, and I will shoot you dead, Odessa."

They were excellent marksmen, right? Professionals go through extensive training. They couldn't possibly miss Odessa and kill her instead.

Odessa's gun hand twitched. The trigger inched back. And then consciousness slipped away.

Chapter Twenty-Five

Alena woke to the odor of ammonia. She pushed it from her nose, but it came right back. She pushed it one final time and opened her eyes.

"That's better." Nan sat back on her heels.

Sam held Alena in his arms on the floor of the conference room, his back resting against the wall. Odessa was on the floor, part of her brain splattered on the conference table. Swarms of cops and plain suits crowded the room.

Nan reached over and gave Alena a kiss. "Scary stuff. I'd beat Sam up for causing all this, but since he's holding you, I'll wait." She palpated Alena's neck. "I don't feel anything out of place, but boy, are you going to have a nasty bruise." She glanced from one to the other. "You both have an awful lot of explaining to do."

"We'll have plenty of time for that," Sam said with a tired grin. He kissed Alena's hair.

"Wait a minute!" she cried, breaking free of his arms and turning. "Did I hear two shots?" She pressed all over his chest. "Did she hit you?"

"No, but your conference room wall has a bullet hole in it. You might have to hang a picture to cover it." He drew her back into his arms. "You no doubt heard the shot fired in the hall. Odessa killed Joe outright. Put a bullet right into his heart. It gave her the few seconds she needed to run back in here and grab you."

Nan grunted. "If you two lovebirds don't need me, I'll return to the ER. Alena can fill me in later." She touched Alena's arm. "Are you really okay? We can get a neck x-ray."

"I'm fine." She rubbed her throat. "That damn woman almost crushed my trachea!"

"That's why she's on the floor with half her brain missing," Sam said. "You were turning blue."

"No thanks to you," Nan snapped. She jumped to her feet. "Call if you need anything." She left.

The medical examiner arrived, followed by CSI, more police, and of course, hospital administration. Alena watched the array of people with a blank mind. She stayed in Sam's arms. If he didn't want to move, neither did she.

"I'm sorry you got involved in all this," he said. "When Odessa ran in here and not the stairwell, I almost lost my breakfast."

"Her high heels prevented a quick escape down a stairwell, Sam. She had no choice but to grab me." She rubbed her neck. "I should have rolled under the table when the yelling started."

He squeezed her tight. "I love you so much. If anything happened to you—" He choked on the words.

"But nothing happened to me because you were here to prevent it." She reached up and brought his lips to meet hers. "Thank you," she whispered.

The reality of the scene was testimony to the danger she faced. Johnny had placed her in grave peril. She would never forgive him.

"You got a text message and then disappeared," she said. "What did it say?"

Sam showed her the message. *BB in lobby.*

Heading your way.

Alena looked at him, puzzled. "BB?"

"Big boobs. It was our code name for her. Rather appropriate, don't you think?" He put his phone away. "The only reason for her to be in the hospital was the card. I asked Tommy if anyone came down here. He confirmed that the security guard, Joe, hung around for a while before hurrying off with his cell phone to his ear. Joe followed every move you made within the hospital walls, Alena. He saw them find the package and ran down. Thanks to Tommy, he stopped Joe from taking it. I disappeared because we needed Odessa with the card in her hand." He buried his lips in her hair. After a time, he continued.

"Odessa had Joe wrapped around her finger. He placed the security cameras in x-ray for the sole purpose of watching you. We tapped into those cameras when we discovered Joe on her payroll. My partner, Dave, the man with the nice head of hair, had instructions to maintain a visual on you at all times. We knew somehow, somewhere, you were the key to the memory card."

"So, all this time, Dave was like a bodyguard."

"Yes, Odessa was dangerous. Quite a few of her men disappeared without a trace——like Johnny. The woman's a cold-blooded killer."

Dave approached with a big grin on his lips. He squatted beside them.

"All this time, the two of you were working together," she said with amazement. "That's why you came up behind me in the parking garage. What did you do with the mugger?"

"Took him straight to headquarters. He was

Odessa's man."

"Thank you."

"You're welcome, and thanks to you, too. If you hadn't mentioned the security cameras, we would never have pinned our sights on Joe McMann. I have one regret, however."

"What's that?"

"Sam got to you first." He touched her chin and winked at Sam before leaving the room.

"Actually, I would have broken his nose," Sam said.

"The prowler outside my door. That wasn't a cop in the car, was it?"

"No. There was always a car nearby and always a watch on the front and back of your apartment. We couldn't let Odessa get to you."

So many events had happened without her knowledge. And now, it was over.

A tall, distinguished man walked in. He nodded at Sam and then stepped back into the hall.

Sam's arms tightened around her before releasing her completely. "I have to go, Alena. From here on, the card and I get an escort. We'll drive you home if you're ready."

She was more than ready. She wanted out of this room and into some fresh air. Alena had enough excitement to last a lifetime.

Chapter Twenty-Six

The weight of two years slipped away as Alena dressed for work the next morning. The answer to Johnny's disappearance freed her heart of the pain that had festered into an anger she could not dispel. She actually whistled while she dressed. A rarity these days especially since she couldn't whistle worth a damn.

Then, of course, there was Sam and his wonderful lovemaking. For the first time in two years, a renewed sense of self hit. She was lucky to be alive. Before she left the bedroom, she put her cane in the closet. She wouldn't need it anymore.

She hadn't seen Sam last night. The Feds had dropped her off without ceremony and sped away to headquarters. A strange sense of loss had sunk in as the car disappeared from the complex. Her adventure was over. Odessa was dead, the memory card in safe hands. Everyone was happy.

Almost everyone.

Doubts surfaced as she left for work. The database belonged in California. Would Sam deliver it personally? Would he stay and never return? If so, their relationship would end before it started. She hoped he at least gave her a phone call before heading back to California. His home. Where his family and job were.

Dammit to hell.

As she pulled into the parking garage, she reflected

on Johnny and his double life. He was such a good doctor, a man full of tremendous self-control. He rarely had shown emotions except when he was with children. How did Odessa get her claws into him? It couldn't be money. He was part of a busy practice and had made his fair share of green. Sex then?

A ridiculous assumption. John Goodhart had considered himself the greatest lover in the world so he had no need for the lessons of a whore. In reality, he was a distant lover, a man too self-absorbed to worry about a partner in bed. Of all the times they had slept together, she reached climax once. Even then, he caused a mere tingle.

Looking back, he had harbored secrets. Those secrets had created mood swings that whipped from happy to dread, from serious to hyper, all within the space of a day. She never knew what to expect when he came through the door. Something had bothered him, and as hard as she tried, she could never get him to talk. Because of this secrecy, they had kept their lives separate even after their engagement, maintaining their own apartments for the sake of sanity. His request more than hers. She had agreed to it however puzzling it seemed. At one point, she had contemplated calling off the engagement since his moods were so strange. She understood why now.

The x-ray department was pretty much back to normal when she arrived. A clean-up crew had torn out the rug in the conference room and were in the process of installing a new one. The CEO and Julius Hoffman supervised from the doorway as if they installed carpets every weekend as a side job. In truth, neither one of them knew how to use a push broom.

Work was a joke. She had a hundred x-ray reports to get out, but everyone and their cousin wandered in for a detailed synopsis of her adventure with Odessa. At eleven when everything calmed down, Sam walked in followed by the distinguished man from yesterday.

They were two men at opposite spectrums: Sam, beefy and muscular, comfortable in blue jeans and flower shirts. The other man had manicured nails and a suit tailored to fit a large frame. Gray hair touched his temples and not a curl was out of place.

Sam kept his distance. No hug, no kiss. His persona was all business. Neither one of them looked glad to see her.

"This is Mike Donovan," Sam said. "He's in charge of the case here in the Philadelphia bureau. Is there someplace private where we can talk?"

"Sure," she said, puzzled. "Follow me." She led them to her office. She turned to face them after she shut the door. "All right, gentlemen, what's wrong?"

She wasn't born yesterday. They looked serious and suspicious. She expected them to whip out handcuffs and haul her in.

"We want you to look at the video on the card," Sam said.

Alena stepped back, aghast. "It isn't really photos of Johnny and Odessa, is it?"

Sam gave her a strained smile. "No. It's a message from Johnny to you."

She jerked. "A message? Sam, I had nothing to do with his activities. You should know that by now." She stopped. She glanced from Mike Donovan to Sam and back again.

"Sam told me everything," Donovan said. "He

knew he broke the rules with you, and he was honest about it."

"Is he in trouble?"

"Not yet anyway. I'm willing to overlook his indiscretion if this case reaches a successful conclusion. So, look at the video and tell us what you think."

"I gather it's not the database."

Both men shook their heads.

Mike Donovan opened a small laptop and placed it on the desk. Her fiancé, John Goodhart, popped onto the screen. She choked at the sight of his face, so alive. She would never see him again. She sat down.

"This video is for you, Alena. If anything should happen to me, I want you to know that I have loved you from the first day we met. At this taping, you are in the hospital, post-op brain surgery. I'm praying I'm at your bedside when you wake up, but there is a good possibility I won't be. I mailed this packet to the hospital because I know you won't be returning to your apartment anytime soon. I hope someone at the hospital has enough sense to lock up your mail."

Well, of course, that didn't work. The package got knocked behind the cabinet. If she hadn't pushed for a cleaning...

"I'd like to apologize for several things, Alena. One, I'm sorry I never got you my mother's brownie recipe. I know you loved it, but she passed away and never wrote it down. Two, I deeply regret not noticing what was happening that night. I was in one of my self-absorbed moods and after my own satisfaction. My problems were coming down on me fast, and I never gave a second thought to the woman lying by my side. That, more than anything, I will regret for the rest of my life." He paused in an attempt to control himself. After a few deep breaths, he continued.

"The third and most important apology concerns your skill as a radiologist. I questioned your ability to read my knee x-rays. Instead, I went to old man Hoffman who can't see worth a damn. I know I hurt you, and I am truly sorry. I should never have doubted your skill. I love you, Alena. I always will."

The video ended. She reached for a tissue to dry her eyes. The two men stood watching her. She didn't care. She blew her nose.

"The database is not on this memory card," Donovan said. "We were hoping Johnny gave you an idea where it might be."

She tossed the tissue in the trash, giving herself time to absorb the contents of the video. Johnny did indeed send her a message. "Well, I'll be damned. I know where he hid it."

She led them down the hall to a cubbyhole of a room where a young woman rushed around with arms full of brown x-ray envelopes. Her poor hair was frazzled and sticking out in all directions as if the envelopes attacked her somewhere along the way. She looked at Alena with something akin to despair.

"Sandy, I know you're busy, but it's important that you get me John Goodhart's knee x-rays."

"Is he an in-patient, Dr. Nichols?"

"No. They should be in the back room."

The young woman's round eyes flicked from Alena to the two men flanking her sides. "Okay. Give me a few minutes."

While they waited, Sam touched her arm. "Explain."

She faced both men. "I thought it odd that Johnny apologized for something that wasn't true. He never questioned my ability to read x-rays. When he twisted his knee, he refused to let Dr. Hoffman read them. For him to say differently must mean that the card is within that folder. If not, then he left another clue for where to look."

Sandy returned with a brown x-ray envelope. Alena thanked her and took out the films. She looked inside the envelope. There, taped to the side of the envelope, was the memory card.

No one jumped for joy. The two men were as serious as ever as Donovan reached in and ripped the card out. They left without fanfare, and she stared after them, feeling a strong sense of loss creep in again. Seeing Sam's serious expression brought it to the forefront. The job was over. She was an assignment, a key to a mystery that would save the United States Government. Hoorah, hoorah!

Slap me now, dammit.

Big deal, they fell in love. How many other assignments had ended like this? Goodbye, farewell, nice to know you, ma'am. The thought hurt. It gnawed in her gut and gave her acid reflux. Why couldn't she meet a man who wasn't hiding behind a charade?

And Johnny. She had wanted some sort of explanation as to why he got involved with Odessa. Deep down, she believed him to be a good man, one with morals and a strong sense of duty.

She pushed both men out of her mind by burying herself in work.

Chapter Twenty-Seven

A few hours later, a shot of déjà vu hit. Alena turned to see Sam standing in the doorway of the reading room. He looked frustrated and a bit angry. She cocked an eyebrow at him.

"Johnny's playing a cat and mouse game with us," he said though tight teeth.

That shot her brow up higher. "What do you mean?"

"Can we go back to your office?"

Surprised, she led the way then realized no one else was behind him. "Where's Donovan?"

"I'm alone this time. If Johnny keeps us on this wild goose chase, Mike thought your concentration might be better without him breathing down your neck. I've got two agents waiting in the lobby, however, in case we figure all this shit out."

She closed her office door behind him. He placed the laptop on her desk and motioned for her to sit.

She hesitated. "This isn't easy for me, Sam. You know that."

"Yes, I do." He wrapped his arms around her and held tight. The gesture did little to alleviate the anxiety, nor did it give reassurance for a relationship teetering on the edge. He kissed her hair before releasing her. She sat down, and he opened the laptop.

Johnny's video popped onto the screen. She

touched his image this time while Sam sat on the corner of the desk, watching.

John Goodhart smiled. "I see you got my first clue, Alena. I want to explain a few things about Odessa." He scratched his ear. He looked nervous. No, maybe the word was guilty. True confession time.

"While I was still a resident," he began, "she approached with an offer too good to pass up. You know, of course, that my father refused to help with my tuition, and I was heavily in debt. Odessa offered to pay that debt if I would do one little job for her. Before I realized, I was involved in a business that would put me away for years." He shifted on his seat.

"When I met you, I wanted out of the business. I agreed to do this last job, and she agreed to find someone else to take my place. Well, she didn't like my leaving at all. The fact that you are viewing this video proved me right. I'm obviously dead, and you are following my trail of clues." He paused to drink from a water bottle. When he looked back, his eyes were intense.

"If Odessa is with you now, I am very sorry. We stole something valuable, and she will stop at nothing to get her hands on it. It's a database downloaded from the U.S. Treasury's computer system. The information will make her a very rich woman." He sat back in his chair.

"When Odessa and I went to Vegas to buy this database, I made a switch before handing it over to her. I kept the real memory card and gave her a blank one. She hit the roof, of course, but it was my insurance to get home alive. I knew I was on borrowed time so I had to act quickly. Despite your stroke and its outcome, I created this trail of cards that only you could follow.

What you do with the final card is up to you. I'd prefer you return it to the U.S. Treasury from where it came along with this video."

Sam stopped the computer. He lifted Alena's chin. "Johnny put your life in danger by what he did. Odessa wouldn't hesitate to put a bullet in your head afterwards. I hope you realize that."

She nodded. "He wasn't sure if I'd survive my stroke either. He should have sent everything back to the U.S. Treasury."

"It would have made my job easier and kept you out of danger." He restarted the video.

Johnny leaned forward toward the camera. "Here's your next clue, Alena. I want you to think of my favorite place. There, you will find the clue to the final card."

The video ended. She sat back and stared at the blank screen.

"Cape May?" Sam asked.

She shook herself and looked up. "What?"

"Was Cape May Johnny's favorite place?"

"Oh, heavens, no. He hated the beach. We never went there together." Her memories of Cape May would always be with Sam. That one day had changed her entire existence. Unfortunately, he was another man who lived a double life. Any future visits to the shore should trigger a sense of irony.

"What's Johnny's favorite place?"

She slumped in the chair. "Disney World."

Sam jerked. "Are you serious?"

"Yes. It was his favorite place. As if he truly left everything behind, not a care in the world. We went down there twice, and he acted like a kid on holiday.

He liked—" She stopped. She stared at Sam with wide eyes. "He liked Thumper, Sam! I gave him a Thumper doll for Christmas! It was in his apartment!"

His brow puckered. "We found his apartment stuff in storage. Odessa ransacked everything." He took out his cell phone. "I'll have the men check it anyway." He made his phone call.

It annoyed her that Johnny involved her in all this. Damn friggin' ass. He would be alive today if he had gone to the cops.

Sam finished his call. "The Goodhart family had wealth. Johnny's father had big-time political connections. Why did Johnny need money?"

"Because Johnny's father wanted him to go to law school. From when he was in diapers, his father groomed him to be a politician, the next president of the United States. Johnny wanted nothing to do with the political life. Like me, he rebelled. His father resented it and cut him off. Johnny had less of a childhood than I did. That's why he fell in love with Disney. We had a lot of fun when we went down." She rested her head back on the headrest and closed her eyes. "We were two of a kind. We both had a parent who wanted their child to live their life." She fell silent.

His cell phone rang. He slipped off the desk to answer it. After a short conversation, he hung up. "Thumper's been ripped to shreds. Can you think of anything else?"

She shook her head. Not a damn iota. Her mind was a blank.

"Think."

"I am," she lied. Then anger set in. She glared at him. "I didn't ask for this, Sam."

He squatted next to her chair. "I know, sweetheart, but Johnny involved you. He made you the key in a very dangerous game. We need that key to get the database. Without you, it may one day fall into the wrong hands." He touched her arm. "It's out there, Alena. The videos prove it. Johnny's left us the clues. We've got to find it."

His phone rang again. He stood up to answer then whirled back to grab the computer. He typed. "Got it!" He ended the call.

"What now?" she asked, startled.

"Our IT techs were trying to break the password on a secondary file. They just gave it to me." He shot her a wry grin. "The word was Thumper."

She never realized Johnny was so good with computers. This from a man who had trouble starting his car.

Sam hit a button, and Johnny's face again appeared.

"By now, Alena, you realize that the final memory card will be hard to find. You alone will find it. If Odessa is standing behind you, take the bullet, honey. She will kill you anyway once she has the card in her hands. Don't let her have it." He sat back. "I gave you the clues. There are no more so I bid you farewell. I love you, Alena. Do me one last favor and tell Daniel goodbye. I'll miss you both."

The screen went blank.

She sat there stunned. He created a password for this? She couldn't make heads or tails of any of it. "Did he go to Disney World after my stroke?" she asked.

"We found no evidence of him leaving the city. Who's Daniel?"

"His Uncle Daniel, I guess. He helped Johnny when Johnny's father disowned him."

"Do you know where he lives?"

"He's dead, has been for several years."

"His gravesite then. That has to be it, Alena." He knelt beside her. "Where's he buried?"

"I've no idea."

"What's his last name?"

"Goodhart. I think he was his father's brother. I never met his uncle. Johnny talked about him, that's all." She stared at the blank screen. "What does he want from me?"

Sam stood to his feet. He sat on the edge of the desk, leaned down, and lifted her chin. Warm lips touched hers. When he pulled away, he said, "Johnny wants you to remember something buried deep within your subconscious. Relax and close your eyes for a few minutes."

The weight of the world fell on her shoulders again. This morning, she had awakened to a wonderful feeling of freedom. Now, a trapped sensation sank in. Somewhere in her brain was the answer to Johnny's puzzle. What did his favorite place have to do with his late uncle? She saw no connection whatsoever. *Why did you have to involve me, damn you?*

A knock sounded on the door. Patty, an x-ray tech, poked her head in. "Excuse me, Dr. Nichols. They need you STAT in ultrasound."

Alena stood to her feet. "Sam—"

"I'll wait here," he said. "I'll see if I can find where Daniel Goodhart is buried."

She touched him on his cheek and followed Patty down the hall.

She needed a distraction. What if her stroke destroyed this one crucial memory? She had no clue what to make of Johnny's favorite place. Sure, he loved Disney. He especially loved Thumper. And what about Daniel? Daniel and Thumper. Disney, Thumper, and Daniel. What was the connection, dammit?

Maybe Sam was right. Maybe Johnny hid the card at the gravesite. If so, that was out of her hands and up to Sam. She entered the ultrasound room.

Forty minutes later, she returned to her office to see Sam sitting at her desk, staring at the small laptop. He looked up as she entered.

"Johnny's uncle was cremated. We checked Johnny's apartment stuff for an urn. Nothing." He sat back in the chair. "Why Thumper? Guys usually relate better to pirates or action heroes."

She sat on the corner of the desk this time. "I'm not sure. We saw *Bambi* together. He loved how all the animals were like babies in the forest. I guess it has something to do with his lost child—"

She shot to her feet with a whirl. "Baby!" She grabbed Sam's arm. "Daniel was to be the name of our first born male!"

He stood to his feet, eyes sharp and alert. "All right. Go on."

"It's been so long. I almost forgot." She headed for the door. "Let's go!"

Sam grabbed the laptop and followed. "Where to?"

"Pediatrics."

"Why?" They headed for the elevator.

"Thumper ears, Sam! Johnny wore Thumper ears whenever he examined a pediatric patient." She hit the button for the pediatric floor.

When they exited the elevator, she headed straight to the nurse's station. A jolly, round-faced nurse smiled up from the desk.

"Dr. Nichols! It's been a long time since you paid us a visit!"

"Hi, Josie. Do you still have Dr. Goodhart's Thumper ears?"

Surprise showed on the round face. "Funny you should ask. Sally's been wearing them for the past week. She's wearing them now. Room five."

Alena led the way. They reached room five as a little boy came running out in his jammies, laughing and giggling. A nurse wearing Thumper ears ran after him. She scooped him up.

"Oh, no, you don't," she told him.

Alena and Sam approached.

"Sally, we need the Thumper ears," Alena said.

Sally bowed her head toward Alena. "Take them. This little guy is a handful."

Alena took the ears and turned to Sam. "Someplace private?"

"Definitely," he said.

She led him to an empty exam room. Sam grabbed the ears and finger-pressed up and down the fuzzy material. His eyes brightened. "Bingo!"

He took out a penknife and cut. The memory card fell out and into his hand.

Chapter Twenty-Eight

They found the database. Sam confirmed it, and they hugged in celebration. After several kisses, Alena escorted him to the lobby, and from there, he joined the two agents waiting.

It was over.

A few days passed without a word. Technicalities, she knew. The shooting death of Odessa. Reports. Briefings. She received the good news at work, which she wanted to share. She debated calling him but decided against it. He had enough on his mind.

And so did she.

The news media had a field day with the story. Mike Donovan gave the interview and revealed the details of the case. The reporters focused on Odessa with her long history of breaking the law. Agent McCullen had his moment before the camera and explained the process of tracking the perpetrators to the east coast. Alena Nichols was a minor player in the drama. Donovan's words, not hers. Certainly not her interpretation. The reporters requested an interview, but she declined. She wanted to put the whole incident behind her.

Sam knocked on her door two nights later. Without a word, he swept her into his arms and carried her straight to the bedroom. His mouth smothered her with kisses as he stripped every stitch of clothing off her body.

She pushed on his chest. "Hello to you, too."

That put a smile on his lips, but those were the last words verbalized. He suckled and tasted every square inch of her body, taking his time and savoring. She whimpered as his hands worked their magic, and he entered with a thrust that nearly put her into the headboard. She climaxed with a muffled howl. His teeth searched and found both nipples before slipping to her side.

They stayed in a tight embrace for the longest time. No words passed between them. Just a reaffirmation of their love for each other. After she listened to his breathing and counted the heartbeats in his chest, she propped herself onto one elbow and touched his cheek. "You didn't have to do this, you know. You look tired."

"I am, but I couldn't think of anything else since we left the hospital. It took everything I had to concentrate during the inquisition. There's always someone on the review panel who believes talking a person down would do the trick. It's usually a desk jockey who reads reports all day. I can tell you, sweetheart, when you turned blue, I lost it. I don't have a second of regret about shooting her either." He fell silent. Alena put her head on his shoulder.

"Ballistics matched the bullet in Johnny's head to a series of murders, a 9mm," he said finally. "Odessa's gun, a .38 special, was matched to a two-year-old cold case in West Philly. This confirmed our theory that Odessa's crony killed Johnny. Then Odessa killed him. She had no choice but to go after you. Alena—" He lifted her chin. "Johnny's body is in the morgue. His father wants nothing to do with him. Should I release him to you?"

She nodded. "I'll see that he gets buried." She toyed with his nipple. "I don't understand how Johnny expected me to access the secondary file. I'm not a computer wiz."

"Oh, I don't know. You're a smart cookie. You would have tried the word Thumper. It's also possible he was forcing you to seek help. He had to know that the Federal government was on his tail. He deliberately looked up at the Vegas cameras to give us a good shot of his face. You may have solved it without his last clue, but if you didn't, we would have been right behind you. The clues were for you, Alena. If Odessa put a bullet in your head, then she would never have found the card. In essence, Johnny gave us enough time to catch up."

She propped herself on an elbow again. "He was protecting me?"

"I wouldn't go that far. He's the one who put your life in danger in the first place. For that, I will never forgive him." He fell silent.

He was troubled.

It showed in his eyes.

She also suspected what it could be.

"I'm leaving for California tomorrow," he said. "I need to complete the paperwork for the case and go through more inquisitions. It's the part of my job I like the least."

He had warned her that he would go back, and he meant it. Now that his undercover assignment had reached its conclusion, nothing should keep him here. Except her. Even that wouldn't be enough. She braced herself for this moment, but it still hurt.

"When will you be back?" she asked. She didn't want to hear his answer.

"I want you to come with me, Alena, as my wife. I want us to be together forever."

She pulled back, a defensive move to prepare for the inevitable. "Rather short notice, Sam. I accepted the promotion at the hospital."

"You're an experienced radiologist. You'll find another position in LA."

She moved away from him. "I'd like to give this one a try first."

He frowned and fussed with the sheet. "You seem reluctant. Did your feelings for me change?"

She took a few moments to answer, a few moments too long. He looked at her with a face full of doubt.

"I still love you very much, Sam, but you must realize that I fell in love with a banker, a man with a nine-to-five job, a man who will be home for dinner, play with the children, and have barbecues, all the good family stuff. Now, you tell me you work undercover assignments, some for months at a time. You want to remove me from the environment I know best, leave all my friends and contacts to start fresh with a man who won't be there. Our marriage will fall apart like your first one. I don't want that to happen. So yes, I am reluctant to marry you. I don't want to live with the constant worry, the constant loneliness—" She paused and met his eyes. "The abandonment."

He studied her in silence.

"You know I'm right, Sam. The marriage is destined to fail."

"My family will be there."

"But did that help your first wife? Did she run to

them every time you went away? My guess is no. Most women will put on a happy face even when their insides are being torn apart. Her drug use was an escape, something to occupy her mind while her world crumbled around her. It takes a special woman to survive that kind of marriage, Sam. I am not that special woman."

He watched her in silence.

She had a longing to throw herself on him one last time, give him anything he wanted to keep him by her side, but she sensed a wall rising.

The relationship had reached an impasse. His job and a continent had come between them.

He slipped out of bed and dressed. "Maybe you would like to come for a visit," he said. "You'll love LA, Alena. A lot of sunshine, perfect weather." He paused for effect. "And a blue ocean."

She smiled at the last part. He leaned over to kiss her. It was a goodbye kiss, one final connection. She would never see him again even for a visit. Alena wanted to cry, but she wouldn't. It wouldn't be the last thing he saw her do.

He stood watching her, his face contorting with hurt and indecision. "I can't say goodbye, Alena."

"Neither can I."

He paused in the doorway. He met her gaze. "You have my phone number if you change your mind."

"Take care of yourself, Sam." She choked on the words. She didn't want him to go, but she knew he wouldn't stay, not even for her. His job was his life.

"I'll lock the door on my way out," he said.

"Sam—"

He turned back.

"Thank you…for everything."

He nodded and left.

When the door bolted shut, the words slipped out of her mouth. "Farewell, my love."

She buried her face in her pillow and let the tears fall.

Chapter Twenty-Nine

Alena put her heart back together. A little glue and duct tape did the job along with a lot of work to occupy her mind. The duct tape had needed reinforcement when she stepped out the door one morning and spotted the moving van in front of Sam's apartment. Reality was a hard pill to swallow.

How many times in life must a woman mend a broken heart? Was there a set number written down somewhere before happiness stayed? She'd like to meet an expert for some answers. She sure as hell didn't have any.

Labor Day came and went. Fall meandered in with its shorter days and cooler nights. Well, no, the cooler nights weren't happening. She had yet to turn off the air conditioner. If the heat insisted on sticking around, she might be wearing shorts for Thanksgiving.

It was one of those in-between days when Alena found herself sitting on a bench across the street from the hospital. The auxiliary had built a cozy little alcove for family and friends of patients. A relaxing place, shaded and away from the sidewalk traffic. The perfect spot to have a private conversation with a woman who grew grumpier and more irritable with each passing day. The cause was as plain as a bird in the tree. Making her friend realize it would take an act of congress.

Nan soon emerged from the front entrance and ran across the street. She flopped onto the bench. She looked tired, and yes, irritable.

"This is unusual," Nan said. "What's up?"

"You. A few nurses from the ER paid me a visit in Radiology. Their complaint was you."

Nan stared. "Me?"

"You've become unapproachable. They describe you as a cyclone that won't stop. They're afraid you'll burn out and stick them with asshole Peters as the primary ER doc. It's clear you aren't handling your sexual frustration very well."

Nan groaned and curled up on the bench. She clamped her arms around her legs and put her head on her knees. After a few minutes, she lifted her head.

"Do you realize I haven't slept with a man in months?"

Nan made it sound like a capital crime. "That's a record for you." Alena suppressed a grin. "I guess the problem is still Nathan."

Nan groaned again and plunked her head onto her knees. "Why does the guy have to be so damn nice?"

"What did he do this time?"

Nan lifted her head and stared off in the distance. She looked lost and undecided. A first for her.

"I came home from a night shift last week and found him sitting on my front porch. He had coffee and donuts." She stopped.

"And?"

She took another minute to continue. "It was a beautiful morning. We sat on my porch rocker and ate." Nan looked at her. Her expression was shy, another first. "When we finished, he put his arm around me, and

I fell asleep. I woke up seven hours later in my bed with my shoes off. He was gone. I've never experienced that."

"What?"

She shrugged. "You know."

"Yes, I do, but I need to hear you say it."

Nan stared down the street, her eyes far away, seeing nothing, not even the good-looking dude walking toward them.

"Trust," she said at last. "I felt an overwhelming sense of trust. I've never felt that with any man."

"Is this over and above the day he took you to the community center?"

She frowned. "In addition to. The man makes me feel so damn...special."

Alena knew what her friend felt because she, too, experienced that wonderful feeling. With Sam.

Gad, she missed him. She had gotten used to having him around. His smile, his touch. The swagger when he walked. A profound emptiness filled her days, and unless she changed her mindset, that emptiness would continue. "It's an indescribable feeling," she murmured.

Nan agreed. "I don't understand it at all."

"That's because you never fell in love."

Nan's face contorted with agony. "Noooo!" she said with a whine. "Shit, shit, shit!" She plunked her head back onto her knees. "I don't have time to fall in love. Relationships take effort. And commitment. Lots of commitment."

"Sometimes it hits when we least expect it. I wasn't looking to fall in love with Sam, but it happened." Now all she had to do was get over him.

She touched Nan on the arm. "Look, honey. If you can't handle what you feel for Nathan, then you need to re-channel your frustration. The ER staff is ready to strap you in leathers and shoot you up with Valium. Why don't you see where your relationship goes with Nathan?"

"I don't want to." She mumbled it into her knees.

"You lectured me about taking a chance with Sam. I'm doing the same to you. Nathan is not your father."

"You don't know that."

"Neither do you. Face it, you don't know a whole lot about the man, and you won't unless you let the relationship run its course."

Nan lifted her head and glared. "Since when did you become a philosopher?"

"I don't want the staff to boil you in oil. You're my best friend."

Nan's face softened and the glare disappeared. Her shoulders relaxed a little. "I'll explore my relationship with Nathan when he gets a job, a *real* job. I will not fall into my mother's pattern of supporting a man until death. I made that promise to myself a long time ago, and I do not intend to break it. My mother married my father when he was unemployed, and he stayed unemployed. I will not become my mother!" Determination shot out of her eyes. If she were standing, she'd stomp her feet.

"You said Nathan was a janitor. That's a real job."

"Oh, please. I make more in a day than he does in a month. My salary can support both of us, but I won't let that happen."

"I'm not telling you to marry the guy or to live with him for that matter. Since I've known you, you've never had any semblance of a long-term relationship. Two dates if that, and you move on. You can't get to know a man in so short a time."

Nan grunted. She dropped her knees and turned on the bench. Her body posture indicated challenge, her gaze a trifle too calculating. "Speaking of relationships, have you heard from Sam?"

Alena shook her head. Not a peep. Four weeks passed since he left. No letter, no phone call, nothing. She had no idea if he arrived in California safe and sound. "We pretty much ended our relationship before he left. I don't expect to hear from him."

"I'm sorry, Alena. I thought he was perfect for you."

"He was. His job wasn't." She fussed with her skirt to hide the pain on her face.

Two ambulances raced toward them, lights flashing. They turned toward the ER entrance.

Nan jumped to her feet. "I've got to get back. I'll apologize to the nurses, the doctors, and even the floor sweeper. I'll tell them I suffered from an extended bout of PMS."

"What will you do about Nathan?"

"Avoid him. The man never calls. He simply shows up." She brushed off the seat of her pants. "I'd like to know how he's so aware of my schedule. *I* don't even know my schedule."

"He's infiltrating your life, Nan, like Sam did with me." She cocked her head. "You told Sam to do that, didn't you?"

Nan's mouth fell open. "And Sam told Nathan! Of course, how stupid of me. Well, I've got news for Nathan. It's not going to work. I need a man who is more transparent, no mystery, a guy with a good job and his life in order. Nothing less will do."

"And if you don't find this well-adjusted male?"

Nan looked down at her friend. Her eyes flashed. "I'll buy a dog!"

****

Sam stood on the deck to his sister's beachfront house, marveling at the peacefulness of her surroundings. Waves from the Pacific Ocean crashed onto the shore in a nice steady rhythm, creating a sound both soothing and hypnotic. Blue waves they were, which brought out a sense of irony. Prettier than green, or brown, whatever that color was back east.

Dolphins fed on small fish not far from the shoreline, their fins bobbing up and down. He had watched dolphins that day with Alena in Cape May. She acted as if they were old friends stopping by to say hello. She even called two of them by name. She could have made it up, but it didn't matter. He had more fun with her on that one day than he had a lifetime here on the west coast.

He missed her, missed her smile, her beautiful eyes. Life felt so empty.

Love would do that, fool that he was to let it happen. Love created fond memories. It enhanced feelings, gave one a sense of purpose. He wanted to believe that his job filled him with a sense of purpose. He performed a vital duty to the United States Government, but somehow, the words gnawed at his gut.

His sister, Jennifer, walked out carrying two glasses of iced tea. She handed him one. "I'm glad you stopped by."

He took the glass and sipped. She always made good iced tea. In fact, Jennifer became a very good cook after a childhood of botching up peanut butter and jelly sandwiches. "The inquisition is over," he said. "I've got a lot of vacation time coming."

"Any plans?"

"Not yet." None at all actually. He had no ambition to go anywhere or do anything. Especially alone. Yet, sitting around in his condo had no appeal either. He looked at his sister, the blonde, blue-eyed beauty who turned a lot of heads. "What did you want to talk about?"

"You." She took his arm. "Sit down, Sammie."

She had asked him to come over earlier, but he'd always found an excuse. He didn't want another inquisition. Unfortunately, he was going to get one anyway. They sat in deck chairs that faced the ocean.

"You've been back for a while now," she said. "You seem happy to be home but the sparkle isn't there."

He cocked a brow. "Sparkle?"

"In your eyes, Sammie. You're not happy at all."

He grunted as he sipped his tea. "It was a tough case. It affected me."

"Why? You've been doing undercover work since Dad got you the job. What was so different with this case?"

Sam studied his sister. She was two years younger, happily married with two rambunctious boys, and lived in this spacious house on the beach. The perfect storybook life. He was divorced, lived in a condo close to the office, had a great job that took him around the world, but always felt as if he had no roots. "It was a tough case," he repeated.

"What's her name?"

He couldn't fool his sister. She was too damn astute. "Alena. She was a suspect."

Jennifer's blonde brows shot upward. "Dear Lord! Did you have to lock her away?"

"No. She was the key to the entire operation. We spent a lot of time together."

"And you fell in love. Why isn't she here with you?"

Sam gulped half his tea before answering. "She's convinced the relationship will fail."

"Smart woman. She's right, you know. You were never home long enough to see your marriage disintegrate."

He grunted in answer and gulped the last of his tea. He looked at his sister. "Did Christine ever come over when I was away?"

"I asked her several times, but she always said no. Mom tried, too, but Christine was too miserable for company. I think that's when she started the drugs. To forget, you know. She had a happy marriage once…in the beginning." She twirled the ice cubes in her glass. "Did you bury her?"

"Cremation."

Jen nodded. "We felt terrible when you called. She could have come to us, Sammie." She stared down at her deck. "I'm in the process of clearing her apartment. Did you want anything?"

"What could I possibly want from that woman? She made my life miserable, if you remember."

Two joggers ran along the shoreline and waved. Jen waved back. Sam glared at them. "I'm up for a promotion," he said.

"Wow, great!" She paused. "Isn't it?"

"I'm not sure what it means yet. I haven't accepted."

"I know what it means. More travel, more time away from home, less time to live a normal life." She sipped her tea. "You should stay single, Sammie. That way, you can come and go as you please without worrying about a wife and family. The loneliness might get to you at times, but you'll avoid another nasty divorce." She slammed her sandaled foot onto the deck. "Spider...yuk!" She checked the underside of her sole and made a face. "Family life is nice if you ever get to try it." She scraped her sandal on the deck.

Sam gave her a severe look. "Can we change the subject, please?" Yeah, right. She asked him over for a reason. His sister wouldn't quit until she stressed her point—whatever that was. "I hear Mom is moving in with you."

"She's ready to downsize."

"Hmmpf. She already downsized by selling Dad's house. I resented her a long time because of that."

Jennifer finished her iced tea. She sat forward in her chair, glass clasped in both hands. Her blue eyes probed through to his soul. "Dad's house was a house of pain for our mother."

"What are you talking about? I loved that house!"

"Yes, you and I loved that house, but for Mom, it held bitter memories, memories of loneliness, of raising two children alone, having family functions without Dad, making excuses for why he wasn't there." She put her glass on the table and sat back.

"Mom talked to me a lot, Sam. She told me how

much you remind her of Dad, his work ethics, and his dedication. You and I both know he was never home. He was always off on one of his many assignments. He never went to any of your football games. He never attended any of my concerts. Mom always went alone to cheer us on."

"Dad worked his ass off to support us," he defended.

"He didn't *have* to work, Sam. He *wanted* to work. You know yourself that the assignments are voluntary. Dad volunteered for all of them. It kept him away for weeks at a time—like you." She stared out at the ocean. "It hurts to think that he loved his job more than us. He couldn't even get away to come to my wedding."

More joggers ran by and waved. Jen waved back. She watched them for a long time before she spoke again. "Mom always knew it was never about money. Dad loved to work. His ego fed on the praise, but she came from the old school. She married him for better or worse."

Sam gasped. "She would have divorced him?"

"In another time and another age, yes. So, when Dad died, there remained no question that she would sell the house. The memories were too painful."

"He left her well-off, though."

"Oh, absolutely, but she said she preferred less money and a little more husband. I think every woman feels that way."

Sam sat in silence mulling over his sister's words. Disappointment was a way of life in their house. His father missed his Most Valuable Player award ceremony in high school, the highlight of his football career. His father had promised to teach him how to drive, but Uncle Henry stepped into that role. By the time he graduated college, his father's chronic no-shows had no affect.

If there was one memory he had of his father, it was the proud expression beaming on his face when Sam got the job at the agency. A job his father had pushed for. The traveling got a bit tiring at times. Long flights. Delays. Weather conditions. Then setting up a cover. The isolation of it bothered him more than anything. After the job, he always returned to a handshake at the office and another pat on the back, maybe a few days off but nothing else. Empty condo, empty life.

He had become his father. He had turned into another child living the life of a parent. Like Alena. Only Sam McCullen never rebelled. He had accepted his father's life and never developed a life of his own.

"Mom cried when my marriage fell apart," he said. "I gather she wasn't crying for me."

"No. She cried because your wife did something Mom never could. She called it quits. It's sad, you know."

His eyes flashed. "I don't need pity."

"You won't get it." She draped her legs over an empty chair. "I'm happy with the life I have. You have to be happy with yours. I'm happy to have my brother back in LA, but it's temporary, I know. Your next assignment is around the corner." She shooed a fly off the table. "Do you miss Alena?"

More than he ever believed possible. Every night he went to bed with her on his mind. Every morning, he woke to wonder why she wasn't alongside. Last week, he had driven a buddy home to his desert ranch. Sam damned near bawled at the color of the sand. "We called it off, Jen. I'll miss her until the memory fades."

"Another job should do it. Does she live near her family?"

He shook his head. "She wanted her own life."

"As opposed to you continuing with Dad's?" Jen swung her legs off the chair and jumped to her feet. "You could buy Mom's house. It's a perfect size for you."

He peered up at her. "Perfect for a single man with no family? No thanks. It's too far to commute."

"Right. Work first, life last. Whatever makes you happy, big brother."

For some reason, her last statement annoyed the hell out of him.

Jennifer had made her point after all.

Chapter Thirty

Alena took her time heading home. She debated a quick stop at the gym to keep up the strength in her leg, but a gorgeous evening couldn't be ignored. A slow jog around the park would do wonders to push out the stale air of x-rays from her lungs. Time to get out and socialize anyway.

She missed Sam so much. Anger had helped her get over Johnny. She didn't have that excuse with Sam. She thought of him night and day, even envisioned his image in an x-ray. She had ordered a new set of films to be sure. The poor patient was convinced an alien was growing out of his liver. Alena had to convince him it was a shadow. The whole damn incident had labeled her a piece of fruit.

She pulled into her assigned slot and sat there.

The last month and a half had been hard. Besides Sam, there were Johnny's funeral arrangements. She had buried him without fanfare. Just her, Nan, and a few staff members from his practice. The complex management had repainted Sam's apartment and rented it within a week of his departure. A young family lived there now. She avoided looking in their direction.

Odessa's apartment took longer since the Feds were involved. The buzz in the complex about the slut on the end stretched for weeks. Even little Mrs. Johnson had bubbled with enthusiasm over the story.

A dump truck had hauled away Johnny's furnishings from storage. The Feds asked Alena if she wanted anything, but Odessa had done a number on every piece. If it had cloth, she had ripped it to shreds. She smashed anything breakable. A knife had cut every piece of his clothing like paper through a shredder. Nothing was salvageable.

The government had seized Johnny and Odessa's bank accounts. The grand total came to 9.6 million. The amount staggered her. They did indeed have a very profitable business going.

Alena jumped at the sound of the tap on her window. Her heart flipped at the sight of Sam standing there. Was this for real? Maybe she was hallucinating, a figment of her imagination from a tired brain. No, he was real and waiting with patience. She stepped out.

Words failed her. Memories flooded her mind instead. He looked as handsome as ever. His skin was deeply tanned with blond hair longer than his usual short crop. Still the poster boy for good health. He kept his distance. More than a month separated them, and they were mere acquaintances again.

"Hi." His eyes scanned her from head to toe. "I like the manager look."

She found her voice. "You've lost weight."

"Thirty pounds." He grimaced. "No appetite."

She knew the feeling. Food was devoid of taste. "What brought you back east?"

"A friendly visit."

Yeah, right, and I love hospital cuisine. She cocked her head.

"All right, paperwork. And some other things. We're still friends, aren't we?"

245

Despite her heart slipping into V-tach, she gave him a slow smile. "Yes, Sam, we are still friends." That would never change. He had given her a life back.

"How about joining me for some dinner at Luigi's? I'd like to hear what's been going on with you since I left."

She wanted to jump into his arms, not eat. She debated. "No, thanks." She turned toward her apartment.

He stepped in her path. "I want to talk to you, Alena. I'd rather not do it on an empty stomach. You want me to lose more weight?"

She was hungry, too. Nothing had appealed to her when the staff ordered out at lunchtime. Unfortunately, nothing would appeal to her at Luigi's either.

"Please, Alena." He touched her arm.

His touch raised goose bumps under her shirtsleeve. With it, vivid memories popped into her mind. She still loved him, and the realization filled her with pain. No, she couldn't do it. She shouldn't let him step in and out of her life like this. She needed to cut the strings that tied them together. Yet, she heard herself say, "I'll change first." No harm in a casual conversation, right?

"You look fine."

"I want to get out of my heels. Luigi's is not considered fine dining. Are we walking?"

"I'd like to. It's a nice evening for a stroll."

Yeah, one last stroll before the memories die. She was out of her mind.

Sad to admit, her hands shook as she undressed. A part of her left for California. Now, he was back. Why? To rip her heart into shreds again?

Alena reemerged a short time later in sweatshirt and blue jeans. Sam stood where she left him, hands in his pockets, looking worried and a trifle lost. His face brightened as she approached.

"Can friends still hold hands?" he asked.

Their eyes locked. She held out a hand. He took it with a light squeeze, and they started toward Luigi's.

"Isn't it a little warm for this time of year?" he asked. "I put my air conditioner on full blast in my hotel room."

"The weather can't make up its mind. I'm wearing a sweatshirt so I won't need a jacket."

There. Casual conversation. As expected. They weren't lovers anymore, just friends.

"I bought a house," he said after a block. "I cleaned out my condo and sold off all my stuff. The house will get everything new."

"That's nice, Sam. Congratulations."

"I also got a promotion with a commendation. That means more money."

More travel, more time away from home. Why bother to buy a house?

They strolled along the streets toward the restaurant. He asked about her new position at the hospital, her responsibilities, and her staff. She asked one question about his promotion, but he sidetracked by changing the subject. Which was fine with her. She really didn't want to hear about his job since it depressed her so much.

Sam dropped her hand. She turned to see him staring at the Victorian house that her eyes avoided as they passed. She walked back. "What's the matter?"

"This house is empty."

"Well, I'll be damned," she murmured.

No draperies, no shades, no nothing. Every window bare and exposed. The furniture gone from the front porch. No cars in the drive. It looked empty and alone.

"I want to see what it looks like inside." He sprinted up the walk and onto the front porch. With his hands cupped on the large picture window, he peered in.

"I sure hope it's empty, Sam. Otherwise, they'll report you as a peeping tom."

"It's empty. No furniture, rugs, nothing. Want to look?"

"No." She already knew what the inside looked like. She had mentally decorated the rooms a half dozen times while waiting for the sellers to approve their bid. It pained her to think about it.

"I'm going to try the front door."

Alena gasped. "Sam, you can't do that!"

"Why not?" With his back to her, he tried the door. He turned, wide-eyed. "It's open!"

Oh, God! This could get them arrested.

"Come on, Alena. Let's go inside."

"You're out of your mind."

"Look, if they left the door open, it's not our fault. I'm curious enough to discover why this house was on your wish list. Besides, if you stay out here, someone will see you loitering and call the cops. Come on before we lose what's left of daylight." He jumped off the porch and grabbed her hand. He pulled her up the steps and into the house. "Wow! Look at this place!" He shut and bolted the door behind them.

Yeah, wow. The house had that effect. It echoed

their footsteps on the hardwood floors. It echoed their breaths off the bare walls. An empty, hollow sound. And not the least bit eerie.

The floors and walls looked freshly scrubbed. Not a speck of dust anywhere. A pleasant scent of roses filled the air. A nice touch. "I guess they're about to put it on the market."

"Would you buy it?"

"This house deserves a family, not just me. Let's get out of here." She turned toward the front door.

"Not on your life, woman. We have a great opportunity to look around without a broker tagging along."

"A broker would prevent us from being dragged away in handcuffs."

Wasted words. He disappeared into another room.

More memories surfaced. She and Johnny walking around with a broker. The furniture that gave the house a homey feel. The excitement of a new experience. The exhilaration when the bid was accepted.

The house she almost had.

Alena wandered into the dining room, curious to see if the beautiful mirror still hung over the fireplace. It did. She touched the carved wood.

"That's pretty good craftsmanship," Sam said, reappearing. "Whoever carved it had talent."

Alena agreed. She fingered the single white rose that rested on the mantel. It looked fresh. Not a stitch of anything in the house yet this white rose sat on the mantel. So strange.

"There's some great woodwork in the kitchen, too." Sam disappeared in the direction of the kitchen.

She had loved the kitchen the first time she walked

in. Hell, she loved everything about the house, and to see it again in such fine condition pleased her to no end. She fingered another white rose resting on the kitchen counter. "Someone is expected here. We better go."

He already disappeared. "We haven't seen the upstairs yet."

His footsteps pounded on the uncarpeted staircase to the second floor. What the hell hit this man all of a sudden? He acted as if he overdosed on caffeine.

"It's dark up here," he called. "I wonder if the electric is still on."

Lights brightened the staircase.

Alena groaned. She hoped she had enough money in her bank account to cover bail. "You're taking too many liberties, Mr. Treasury Agent." More wasted words. She climbed the stairs while fingering the intricately carved banister.

A toilet flushed.

"Water's on!" he called.

Great. What next, the central air?

Alena started. *The central air was already on*! "Sam, we gotta get out of here! A realtor with some potential buyers must be coming! I for one do not want to spend the night in jail." A career-buster for sure. "Sam?" She reached the top of the stairs.

The house contained three bedrooms, all on the second floor. The two smaller ones faced the rear of the house. The master bedroom stretched the entire length of the front. Of course, that was the room brightly lit for all the world to see.

"This bedroom has a gorgeous fireplace, Alena! Come and see!"

Yes, she knew it had a gorgeous fireplace. She had

dreamt of nights in bed with Johnny with a roaring fire setting a romantic mood. "I think you stayed out in the California sun too long, Sam. You're acting crazy."

The scent of roses grew stronger as she approached the master bedroom. She entered...and froze.

A large bouquet of white roses sat on the floor in front of a cold fireplace. Next to it stood wine on ice with two crystal-stemmed glasses. Between the two was a small brown envelope.

The two windows had sheets hanging from hooks to allow privacy. And more. Two sleeping bags waited on the floor. Sam watched her from the corner of the room.

"What's going on?" she asked.

Sam put his hands in his trouser pockets before answering. The hyped-up persona had disappeared. There stood the man she knew, a confident man, a man proud of his accomplishments, standing tall and alone. He stepped away from the corner but did not approach.

"When you first showed me this house," he began, "how you loved it, and how it slipped away, I called several real estate brokers and told them I wanted to know immediately if it went up for sale. I had no idea why I made such a move. I never intended to stay on the east coast after this assignment. My home was in LA, and I intended to return."

He meandered to the fireplace and stared down at the roses. "A broker called a few weeks ago. I almost told her to forget it, that my reason for buying the house no longer existed, but something stopped me. I thought I'd sit on the news a bit." He wandered toward the windows. With his back to her, he again spoke.

"When I was a little boy, I thought my dad was a

great man. He worked hard and provided well for my mom, sister, and me. His work meant everything to him, and I admired his strong work ethic. I wanted to be like him in every way." He moved from the window. His face was an emotionless mask.

"Looking back, I realize how little I saw of my father. He was never home. He never took the time to enjoy his family or all that he accomplished to make us comfortable. The pattern repeated with me. Even though my father and I worked at the same agency, I never saw him. I volunteered for assignments, and he did the same. I thought nothing of canceling engagements with my wife or family because the glory of solving a new case always took precedence. My father was the same way." He paused to stare down at the hardwood floor.

"It struck me how I didn't want that life anymore, the constant pat-on-the-back ego trip that my father started when I was barely out of diapers. It was his life, Alena. Like you and Johnny, I became another child living the life of a parent. I never rebelled like you did. I went along with it because I wanted my father to be proud. In following his dream, I never developed a life of my own. A second phone call from the realtor made me realize why I told them about this house. I knew it then, I know it now. The answer is you." He faced her.

Alena stood mute.

"I was angry at first as I flew back to LA," he continued, "angry at you for not being in the seat next to me, angry because you weren't willing to give LA a try. I figured my happiness meant nothing to you, and you had no regard for what I wanted or what would make me happy."

"That's not true," she whispered.

He stopped her. "That was my father talking. My anger grew from a selfishness he instilled early in my career. You told me you moved away from your parents to start your own life. I never did that. My job was a continuation of another man's dream. If I am to break the pattern my father created, then I must put you first. That means returning to the east coast, to the new friends I made, to my new job at the agency, and most of all, to the woman I want to grow old with." He took a few steps toward her.

Alena started. "What new job? Your promotion?"

His lips curled with a faint smile. "Before I left, Mike Donovan took me aside and asked me to stay. I refused because LA was my home, and I thought that was where I belonged. I felt certain you would come with me, but you saw farther into the future than I did. As the weeks passed without you, I grew tired of the emptiness of my life. The pat-on-the-back didn't do it anymore. So, in lieu of a promotion, I requested a transfer back here under Mike Donovan. I also requested to be removed from fieldwork. Mike offered me a financial analyst position, which, in essence, is a promotion. It requires some travel, but nothing undercover and not weeks at a time. I may even drag you along on a few trips." He watched her. "If you don't want the house, I can always put it back on the market."

She shook her head, stunned beyond words.

He approached and put his hands on her shoulders. His touch was light, almost a caress. His eyes showed warmth with a hint of uncertainty. He took hold of her chin. "I wasn't completely honest about Christine's death, Alena. When I looked out the window and saw her in the alley, I realized how wrong I was to marry her. I didn't give her a husband. She got a man too self-absorbed with his career. I'm changing all that for you. So, yes, you're right. This house needs a family, our family. I want to have children to play with as my father never did with me. I want to spend a huge amount of time with my beautiful wife. In order to do both, I need to stay at a job that allows me room to breathe. Working as an analyst gives me that room. I love you, Alena. Nothing will ever change that."

Tears streamed down her cheeks as she looked up at him. "You're changing your life for me?"

He wiped away her tear. "Without a second of regret. You're the best thing that happened to me. For the first time in my life, I feel anchored and ready to stay put. My mom and sister cried when I told them my plans. They were happy tears this time. I was doing something my father never did. I changed my life for the woman I love very much." He kissed her nose. "Open the little envelope."

She did. A key dropped out.

"That's for the front door. We'll change all the locks before we get started if—" He stopped.

She blinked at him. "If what?"

"You marry me."

Tears flowed down in buckets. She couldn't answer if she tried. She nodded instead. He wrapped his arms around her and drew her tight to his chest.

"I missed you so much," he whispered into her hair.

An instantaneous flood of relief swept through her. She melted against him and buried her face in his shirt, sobbing uncontrollably.

After several long minutes, the tears stopped. They stood in each other's arms, neither feeling the urge to separate. "I don't suppose this house has any tissues," she said with a sniff.

"There's toilet paper in the bathroom, but I have a better idea." He lifted her chin and kissed both wet eyes until settling on her mouth.

Her Sammie was back with all the love and tenderness she remembered. She sucked it in without hesitation.

The doorbell rang.

"They've come to arrest us," she mumbled into his mouth.

He pulled away with a big grin on his face. "Dinner. I ordered mushroom pizza from Luigi's. Are you game?"

She was more than game. She was going to spend the rest of her life with a wonderful man.

"Wait a minute." She stopped him from leaving the room. "What's with the sleeping bags?"

He flashed a devilish grin. "I'm sure you can guess. This will be the first night we spend together in our new house."

Food. Then sex. An all-nighter making love. With the man she loved so very much. With a happy shriek, she raced him down the stairs.

Epilogue

Alena stood outside on the sidewalk watching the realtor hammer the For Sale sign into the front lawn. She'd known this day would come. Their family had become too big for the house, and she was pregnant with their third. She sighed.

"Multiple listing in the morning, Mrs. McCullen, although we've got quite a few interested already." He shook the sign to check for sturdiness. "Should hold. Make sure the kids don't pull it out. I'll be in touch."

"Thank you, Mr. Felton."

He drove off with a wave.

Sam pulled into the driveway a few minutes later. She waited for him to join her since she still stood on the sidewalk facing the house. They kissed.

"Inevitable," he said as he checked the sturdiness of the sign. "If the house had one more bedroom, we could have stayed."

"You need an office. You deserve it with your new promotion. In addition, we need a guest room. I'd like to have your mother stay longer when she comes. She's a real gem, Sam. I like her. She's such a contrast from my mother who, by the way, has already tried to dress up our daughter for a parade. Besides, we don't know how many more kids we'll have."

"Three's enough, don't you think?"

"Daddy! Daddy!"

Two small children ran toward him, a boy and a girl. Sam handed Alena his briefcase so he could sweep both into his arms. They kissed and hugged.

"I'd like to see you do that with three kids," she said with a chuckle.

"I might claim back problems before that point." He lowered them to the lawn and off they ran, lugging his briefcase between them. Sam kissed Alena as he wrapped his arm around her shoulders. They headed for the front porch.

"Four," she said. "Nice and even."

He looked at her. "Are you sure?"

"At the moment, yes, but I could change my mind. Our new house has the room."

"Yeah, too bad we couldn't expand here. The yard's not big enough."

"Our new yard is."

He squeezed her. "Don't get any ideas. Four's the limit. We're gonna raise the kids, and then, I want you all to myself again. Got that?"

"Yes, sir." Like she could argue with the man. "Did you really want Donovan's job?"

"I wasn't planning on it. Evidently, he was. He said he groomed me from the day I returned. In a way, leaving fieldwork was the best move I ever made. I should thank you for that." He kissed her tenderly.

"And Johnny. If it weren't for him, you'd be stuck on the west coast."

"Yeah, funny how everything fell into place. When we first met, we asked for nothing in return. Now, we have it all."

He took the words right out of her mouth.

A word about the author...

Jane is a retired respiratory therapist who is married to a wonderful organic farmer. She is an amateur astronomer, an amateur ham radio operator, and an avid people watcher. She loves to hear or read how two people meet, young and old. When she isn't traveling, she lives in southern New Jersey.

Jane can be contacted at:

janedrager@yahoo.com

or visit her website at:

janedrager.com